THEODORE C. VAN ALST JR.

THE EL

Theodore C. Van Alst Jr. (enrolled member, Mackinac Bands of Chippewa and Ottawa Indians) is the coeditor of *Never Whistle at Night: An Indigenous Dark Fiction Anthology*, and the author of the story collections *Sacred Smokes,* winner of the Tillie Olsen Award for Creative Writing, and *Sacred City,* winner of the Electa Quinney Award for Published Stories. His Pushcart-nominated fiction has been published in *Southwest Review, Chicago Review, Red Earth Review, Journal of Working-Class Studies, The Massachusetts Review, The Rumpus,* and *Indian Country Today,* among others. He is a professor of Indigenous Nations Studies at Portland State University.

ALSO BY THEODORE C. VAN ALST JR.

The Faster Redder Road (editor)
Sacred Smokes
Sacred City
The Longest Street in the World
Pour One for the Devil
Sacred Folks
Never Whistle at Night (coeditor)

THE EL

THE EL

THEODORE C. VAN ALST JR.

VINTAGE BOOKS

A DIVISION OF PENGUIN RANDOM HOUSE LLC

NEW YORK

A VINTAGE BOOKS ORIGINAL, AUGUST 2025

Published by Vintage Books, a division of Penguin Random House LLC,
1745 Broadway, New York, NY 10019.

Vintage and colophon are registered
trademarks of Penguin Random House LLC.

The Library of Congress Cataloging-in-Publication Data has been applied for.

Vintage Books Trade Paperback ISBN: 978-0-593-68676-8
eBook ISBN: 978-0-593-68677-5

Book design by Christopher M. Zucker

penguinrandomhouse.com | vintagebooks.com

Printed in the United States of America
10 9 8 7 6 5 4 3 2 1

The authorized representative in the EU for product safety and compliance
is Penguin Random House Ireland, Morrison Chambers, 32 Nassau Street,
Dublin D02 YH68, Ireland, https://eu-contact.penguin.ie.

As always, for Amie, Emily, and Blue

THE EL

If you don't mind the gap in Chicago, it'll swallow you whole. Bonus, they don't tell you there's a gap or even if the doors are closing. Bam. They shut tight and off you go. Better find a space to sit or stand and hang on. Move, my eyes but not my mouth say. Nine point nine times out of ten it's better if you don't talk to people on the El, at least not out loud. Observing my fellow travelers, I'm sure I'd rather not hear what any of them has to say anyway. I grab the overhead handrail as gears grind under my feet, rusty wheels scrape bright stainless tracks while we hump over connections and downed or drunken pigeons, clack=clack=clack, the car swaying at high speed. Gray-enameled back porches and oily red brick hit by splashes of sudden and loud-colored graffiti fly by. I always watch the other passengers' eyes staring through the big filmy windows, track the rapid movement of their eyeballs bouncing and buzzing at every distraction thrown their way. On the Jackson Park–Englewood line, there are thousands. I wonder if my own eyes do that at all the things I see whether I'm on the El, or not. It doesn't seem like it, but I'm buried in them, so I don't really care what the world can't see.

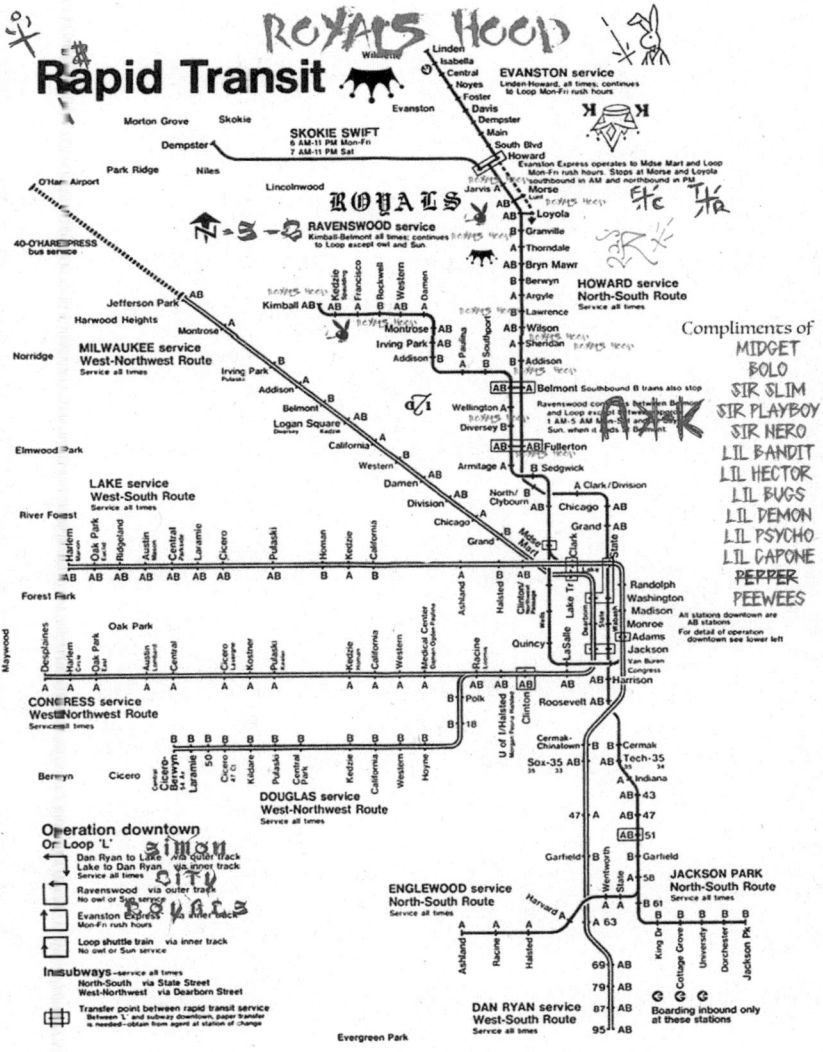

They even came with us to the G/L house on Montrose. A lot later we hung with the SCRs now and then and went on raids with them. I was never really comfortable around them. Some of their guys were alright, but I always had an uneasy feeling with them. There was something that you couldn't quite trust about them. It could have been because they were not all white or not really greasers in my opinion. It seemed like they were more criminally minded. They were also friendly with groups we were not friendly with.

—Anonymous member, Insane Popes (1982)

TEDDY

Folks say they don't want to hear stories start with I woke up, or I was dreaming this, that, and then *all* a that, but I'm telling you anyway that morning I creaked my eyes open to high noon heat and humidity before the sun'd barely dragged its fat summer ass up over the horizon. That's how it's going to start. The box fan filling the window wheezed in damp air a degree cooler than whatever temperature was boiling up in the alley. Any breeze wandering around out there was slo-mo drifting in from Lake Michigan to the east; I smelled piles of dead alewives already baking on the sand at Leone Beach. I'd advise against swimming today if you're heading down to the lake.

Myself, I wouldn't have to worry about stepping over rotting fish to get in some water later. No, this fine August afternoon—in the last summer of the '70s, the first season we'd all started to figure out what those love songs were really trying to say—would see me and a shit ton of Folks from the Simon City Royals V headed to a big meeting called by the C/P/W set, Central Park and Wilson, miles away from the beach.

The way I heard it, the older bros who were locked up made an alliance between the Simon City Royals 🔱 and the Black Gangster Disciples ✡ in the joint and that translated to the same out in the world. Inside and outside we'd be part of the Folks Nation. This new Nation included a lot of our old enemies like the Latin Eagles 🦅 and Imperial Gangsters ♚ and that was a whole new thing we'd have to work out here in the street. On the other side of things, other traditional opposition like the Latin Kings 🦅 and Unknowns ♠ got together to form the People Nation along with all kinds of Vice Lords 🎩, Conservative, Cicero Insane, Traveling, and more. The city was effectively split into two gigantic rival factions, kind of like L.A. with the Crips and Bloods. And the C/P/W branch of Royals was at the center of that treaty-making out here, so that meant we'd be heading out to their hood and Roosevelt High School for a meetup. Say *Rooooosevelt*, if you want to pronounce it Chicago-style, at least in my neighborhood. Johnny Miller was calling the shots and they said CoCo from the west side Black Gangster Disciples ✡ would be there to tell the whole set what was up. I hoped someone would be looking out for me, for us—Jesus, Coyote, Al Capone, whoever had a minute to spare, it didn't matter—I was sure all of us prayed to them equally.

I walked into the kitchen, grabbed the short I had left in the ashtray last night, lit it with a pack of black-and-silver Playboy Club matches that had been lying next to it on the chrome and Formica table. I went to flick off the little light above the stove, but instead turned up the front burner and threw on a tortilla from the pack on the counter. I smoked while I flipped it back and forth, watched it puff up with the hot air trapped inside, smelled the crispy black dots and dashes popping up with each turn. I set my cig next to a different batch of burn marks on the edge of the table and opened the fridge looking for the butter. We had real butter for now 'cause my dad had traded for it—commod cheese and powdered milk or some shit. Otherwise, we'd just have what he called oleo.

I'd been living with him for the last few years after my ma kicked me out for keeping pistols in the house. She came home one night from waitressing at Gullivers Pizza, was like, "I want you out of here after school tomorrow." I had to go to my boy's funeral then come home and pack a Hefty bag, but that's a-whole-nother story. Maybe not all that interesting right now, maybe I already told you anyway, so we'll go with this one here.

The old man was at work, left a couple hours ago, probably still drunk from the night before, but whatever. He never missed work unless he was in jail. How the fuck do you call in sick from the County over at 26th and California? He always did shit that wouldn't get him I-bonded—that's a released-on-your-own-recognizance bond after they bust your balls by making you spend the night in jail—like put people through plate glass windows, but he never lost his job, always made bail. He got popped one time and my ma went to bail him out at the State Street station but spent all her time in the bullpen talking to some Black Panthers who were waiting to get transferred to County or maybe downstate to Joliet or worse. He didn't like that shit, complained about it to me after; she bragged about it to me in a seriously casual way. But anyhow, yeah, he was good at what he did, I guess, was a clerk downtown at the exchanges somewhere, handled physical deliveries for commodities traders—cattle, corn, lumber, pork bellies, gold. I wondered why and how he ended up in that gig, and then I remembered some of our Chippewa and Ottawa ancestors did the same kind of shit back in the old days at Mackinac, trading post stuff. We were half-breed go-betweens, speaking multiple languages, moving goods back and forth. Made sense we'd still do it, why not. And when I found out later that the word *odawa* could mean trader, too, well, yeah.

I found the butter, threw a little on my hothothot-tststs tortilla along with some Tabasco sauce and ate it while I cooked up another one, my smoke forgotten until I smelled a fresh burn mark lining up next to its pals on the table. I put it out and paid attention to this breakfast thing, went over the day ahead. Funny, I could eat breakfast but what I really was only ever thinking about was supper. That meal usually occurred at the best time of the day. Gold light, magic light, it was finally gonna be night, be dark—the time when anything, the best things, could and would happen.

Anyway, I was responsible for this whole show, getting our set out there, making sure we didn't get busted or mopped. It was wild to think how no one else ever thought about this shit, just went about their business no worries, like it would all work out, and they didn't have to give it a second thought. It only worked because of folks like me, but who cared about us? And yeah, it's mostly fine when you're a kid taking care of business and whatnot, but as I'd later learn too many times, when you're all grown and out in the work world as a high school dropout, being used to being in charge can cause some serious performance problems. It's even worse if you go in the service. And they make you take your GED there for nothing.

The phone rang loud on the wall. Fuck. This early in the morning usually meant bad news, but I was gonna stay positive. Big day ahead.

"Hey."

"What up?"

"You see it." It was Mikey1. We had two more Mikeys in the set, but yeah, he was number 1. "What time we leaving?" he asked.

"When I'm ready, fucker." I backed out of the kitchen into the hallway as far as the cord would go, trying to get it to unwind, surprised he called instead of just coming to the crib.

"Pssss," he said, laughed. "Get up, Midget. Let's get going."

"I'm up, man. Even had breakfast." That's kind of a big deal, 'cause I'm a late-night person, always have been, always will be. Didn't even come into this world on my born day until well after noon, so breakfast in the morning was rare. "Head over this way. Bring some smokes."

"Smoke or smokes?" I could hear the music for someone losing on *The Price Is Right* in the background.

"Smokes, man. Don't be getting high until later. We gotta be on top of our shit."

MIKEY

Fuckin' Teddy, telling me not to get high. You know he was drinking already at ten in the morning, the motherfucker, just like his dad. Prob'ly sitting at his kitchen table, having a beer, reading a book, and eating those fuckin' tortillas he loved. I seen him steal 'em by the dozen; his old man wouldn't buy 'em, said they were for Mexicans, and their family didn't eat that shit. His old man could be an asshole, but the lights and the gas were always on, and I could sleep over there whenever I wanted, so it wasn't so bad, I guess. I'm glad they were back to living up here in Rogers Park.

I poke through a bunch of Styrofoam containers in the fridge that my ma stuffed in there yesterday. She works at a Greek restaurant, so no telling what she'll bring home. They make everything there. I remember one night I was jazzed for wings, but when I started eating what I thought was a bunch of flats I figured out they were frog legs, so what the fuck. Yeah, shit *don't* taste like chicken, know what I'm sayin'?

Anyway, I'm about to grab up my smokes and prep up, head to Teddy's house. We got a big day ahead of us. There's an important meeting this afternoon at Roosevelt, the place where the guy who wrote that cool-ass book *The Man with the Golden Arm* went to high school. I snatch my markers and try to get my head right for this. Prob'ly gonna be a quiz later or some shit, the motherfucker. The only thing I feel like studying about right now, though, is hooking up with Juanita later tonight.

TEDDY

Sitting at our kitchen table with the back door open wide, flies already dive-bombing the screen door, some big enough to make it click in the frame, I read yesterday's paper, which the old man had found on the El on his way home. We had a pile of them, especially the Sunday ones.

I loved the newspaper. Also, they would print shit like this, which we thoroughly enjoyed, and which I searched for and clipped obsessively. This one was from the *Chicago Daily News,* I think:

6 ARRESTED AS 3 YOUTHS ARE SHOT IN TEEN FIGHT

Three youths were injured in a single shotgun blast Sunday night and six others arrested in a teenage gang fight in the 3500 block of North Ave.

Some 35 to 40 youths on the scene of the 9:30 p.m. rumble between the rival C-Notes and Simon City gang were questioned by Shakespeare police officers working throughout the night, leading to the arrest of four youths and two juveniles.

Arrested were Daniel Salvo, 20, of 1250 N. Avers, who reportedly fired the blast into the midst of the fight.

(and then blah blah blah names of more dumbasses who got caught, etc.)

Hahaha. *35 to 40 youths.* Nowadays, that shit would be on the national news. Back in the day, though, it was just a *Sunday* night. Even the cops were a little more low-key then.

I listened to the radio, switching between The Loop and WMET Classic Rock when the classic got too Beatles or Stones, smoked the last cigarette in this soft pack, picked at the little glittery flecks in the Formica while I waited. The gold specks made me think of us, stubborn and never going anywhere. Mikey showed up about fifteen minutes later, already shirtless in the heat and humidity. His skinny ass lived a few blocks away across the park and down the street. I went out to meet him at the back porch when I heard him pounding up the stairs. He looked a little high, like he had done a wake and bake and nothing since. We shook hands, Royal-style; soul, then crossed forefingers like guns, hooked those, and twisted them up to pitchforks by adding middle fingers and thumbs, then dropped the middle, touched pinkies, flicked our wrists, threw down the crown.

'Come on in, Folks." I shut the back door on a train going by a few blocks east, the screech of metal and brakes amping up as it slowed for its eventual stop at Howard Street. There wasn't about to be a breeze anytime anyway.

Mikey was a half-breed, too, I guess, but that's not what we called folks who were mixed Black and white. Half-breed was for us Injuns mixed with whatever else. Mikey and his little brother looked mixed yeah, but—crazy—he had two older brothers, one for sure looked just Black and the other straight-up white. You never know what you're gonna get with genetics. Life's a beautiful thing.

From the jump, Mikey was the realest, downest bro I ever had. He was the only cat who would write me when I went in the navy. First in line for everything, the one brother you knew would have your back no matter what. It's funny how you know these things about people and it's never from asking, always from watching.

Keep your eyes on Mikey for two minutes and you'd know what all he was about, no doubt.

"You gotta memorize an address, though." I tilted my head to him, raised my left eyebrow and the same side of my mouth, scratched at this wispy goatee on my chin. "If we get separated and you're walking down the street and the cops pull you over, you better be from around there or they're taking your ass to jail." I slid a Kool 100 from the pack he had thrown up on the kitchen table, reached for those sexy matches.

"How the fuck are we gonna do that? It ain't our hood." Mikey slapped at his chest, rubbed the side of his face, ran a hand over his growing-out-a-little shaved head. He had a big natural for as long as I'd known him but had decided to skin it all off at the start of summer.

"It's the Northwest Side. The neighborhood is a bunch of DPs and Polacks and shit. Just go to Vukovich or Kominski or Pulaski or something in the phone book and pick a address with a N for north in it."

I went and grabbed an Albany Park from the pile of neighborhood white pages I kept on the rickety wooden stand shoved against the wall under the phone. Same as when I first moved in and the old man handed me a map of Chicago, I had memorized the streets in all the neighborhoods we might want to visit. It was the only way to get intel without going in person back in the day. You could see all the parks, the landmarks, even the alleys. Everything you needed to know.

"Here, look: Stanislaus Kowalski, 4542 N. St Louis," I said. "Just do that. Or go to the zip code map and look up 60625 then find a name. It's what I told RJ and Pepper to do."

That RJ? Slide the letters together, pronounce it *Rage,* sometimes.

'What if they check the last name against the address, bro?" he said.

"They ain't gonna do that. They just want to hear something close by, something tells them they won't have to drag their fat asses out of the squad car. There's some hillbillies left over there, too, so don't sweat it you ain't a Polack. Just play it cool, tell 'em your mas from Tennessee. Ain't no way they'll take you for a G/L—you don't look like any kinda Gaylord anyway, but maybe half white trash so you'll be all set."

"Alright, Folks. If you say so. I trust you, Midget."

"Trust me, Bolo. I got you, homes. You want a tortilla or something? You hungry?"

'Nah. I'm good." He was doing the magic trick where it looks like you're spinning a quarter by rubbing along the top of your finger but you're really hitting it with the edge of your thumb.

"Alright."

He loved that trick and so did I. I taught it to him and no one else. He was better at it than I was and none of the boys could figure it out no matter how many times he did it. Hilarious.

I opened the fridge to throw in the tortillas since I'd be gone all day. "Bro. I'm gonna get a beer. You want one?" I had found a couple of Old Styles on the bottom shelf of the fridge and a whole six-pack of Stroh's the old man had hidden under the world's oldest bag of russets. Popcorn-sized potato eyes kept guard over the cold gold cans.

Mikey laughed. "Sksksks, bro, it's like ten-thirty in the morning."

"So what," I said. "Do you want one or not?"

"Pretty funny, Teddy, how you're down on me about not getting high but you're like a hardcore wino or some."

"Man, fuck you. It's just a beer, homes. You ain't gotta drink it. I'm just being polite."

"Calm down, homes. I'm just playing. You got any orange juice?" He smiled.

"Too funny," I said. "There's some powdered shit in the cupboard you can make up if you want."

"Like the milk?" he laughed. "That commodity shit you all get . . . Hey. Got any of that cheese, bro?"

"Shiiiit. The old man traded for some then turned around and sold it. We're out."

"Too bad, homes. It's some good shit."

"You ain't lying. It's some *gold* shit."

I said fuck a beer anyway, slammed the fridge and went down the hall to the bathroom. Steel on steel from train cars at the Howard Street hub screeched through the bottom of the open wire-laced safety window propped up with a stubby clay flowerpot full of dead cigarette butts and an even deader cactus. I took a leak, tried to figure out how else to keep us from getting thrown in jail, have a story for the cops, make sure everyone had tokens for the El, a little cash, no weapons to get them locked up. This meeting was gonna be a big deal, especially for those of us on the city's edge, way up north. Yeah, we had our battles and whatnot with a couple different sets of Latin Kings 👑 and the one branch of Howard Street Lords, plenty of gangbanging sure, but shit, some of those other sets like Unknowns, Deuces 🂡♠, and Gaylords ✠ had to commute to us, or we had to steal a car and drive their way, strapped and ready to go. If we wanted to beat that ass local, we had to scare up some Assyrian Eagles 🦅 over on Devon (that's the avenue pronounced *DuhVAHN*) or Mexican Playboys and Kings down on Howard Street. Sometimes we'd get down with Gaylords in Uptown if your family had money to go school shopping at the Sears, or if you had ties back there the way my family did, Indian or hillbilly or both, like us. When summer came, we could steal a car, head up to Humboldt Park, fuck around and do drive-bys to our heart's content. But the winters got long and quiet and stir-crazy would get you into trouble. Full-on entry into this Nation would keep us busy year-round, make us targets, yeah, but would open up a whole new range of people to humbug with. And you gotta know, I need to put in a disclaimer here, or whatever it's called, this was right before everyone was packing and ready to blaze at the drop of a hat every time, when we still humbugged pretty regularly, getting down in old school . . . rumbles, I guess the real senior brothers called it. Just beating the shit out of each other, no one really dying. Folks packed, yeah, but the guns almost never came out if we were just boxing and whatnot. Good times.

Toilet flushed, I ran my hands under the cold-water tap, shook them out, rubbed the backs on my powder blue cargo baggies and the fronts on my crisp white dago T. I looked down at my black high-tops, webbed up with fat royal blue laces. Your shoes were your flag when you went to other neighborhoods, no way to drop it. That's pretty much the uniform for most of us soldiers. I thought about putting all my hair, which went halfway down my back, in a ponytail just in case, said fuck it, ran my ever-present big gray Goody comb through it a few times, headed back to the kitchen. Even though I'd officially been a warlord for the T/R Peewees and now spent my time with F/C, I kinda kept the job 'cause I had seniority now, helped out with shit. Either way, I had to look good doing it, and today was a good hair day. I'd got up early and showered, so yeah.

"Mikey. You ready to go?"

He was sitting at the table still, rubbing the top of his head, smoking one of his Kools and laughing to himself. He did that a lot. I kind of wanted to know why but liked it a little more that I didn't.

"Yeah, Folks. Let's go," he said, quick-like, always more in the moment than he let on.

"Alright. Grab your squares. And them matches." I had a couple books in my pocket already plus a lighter like always. A royal blue Bic. But they don't last forever. I stood with my hand on the table, waiting for "Samba Pa Ti" to finish. I think it's rude to turn off a song before it's over.

"Come on, Midget. Let's go." He slapped his chest a couple times, shoved the matches in his pocket. He threw me a half pack of Newports in the box.

"Hang on, man," I said, jamming them in my front left pocket.

"For real?" He stood up.

"Yeah." I spun a ring of keys on my finger. I grabbed my gold-framed aviator sunglasses off the table, put them on just so.

"Oh yeah. We gotta wait for the song to end, right?" Mikey said.

"Right."

"Man. You're dedicated to that shit."

"Seriously, bro. It's rude." I put the keys in my pants pocket, front left, under the smokes.

"They ain't gonna know you turned off their shit."

"But *I'll* know," I said. "And it ain't right."

"You're a different kinda dude, Midget." He cracked his knuckles.

"Yeah, well, you gotta stand for some things." The song did the '70s fade. "And for me, this is one of those things." I pulled my shirt off, folded it in thirds, draped it through my belt on the right-hand side. I grabbed the Albany Park white pages, rolled it up, stuck it in my right cargo pocket along with a tube of Krazy Glue, electric tape, two royal blue Flair felt pens, and a loaded Swiss Army knife I traded two joints for with a nerd at school. The left pocket had a copy of Mike Royko's *Boss* in it.

The last note of Carlos's guitar faded into the stratosphere. Mikey smacked both hands on the table. "Alright, Folks, it's over."

"It is," I agreed. "Let's go."

MIKEY

Man, this motherfucker and his tunes and his waiting for songs to end. It was some weird and annoying shit, but I guess it was rooted in respect. And art. Always talking about books and painting and music and all. It was funny, the way he'd go on about that stuff; probably thought he was the only one who cared about it. I liked to read and all, laughed when he'd puff up about some shit he'd read, start running down the finer points. I'd usually already knew it, but I never said anything. Pffft. Bro, you ain't the only one who picks up the newspaper, knows where the library is, likes the big humbug in *Beowulf,* moving out on Grendel and whatnot, or fighting Orcs and shit. It was all good, though. It came from a solid place in him. His old man was kind of a shit so he spent most of his time reading and thinking, taking himself to places where other folks couldn't find him. At least it's what I told myself when he was staring off into who knows where.

TEDDY

We blazed out the back door. I locked up and we tore down the stairs, wanting to be outside more than we realized. We hit the alley and two garages down Mikey pulled out a marker, an old-school Sanford with the good smell.

"Tag it, bro," I said.

"There's a little space here," he said. "Want me to throw you up there, too?"

"Well, yeah," I said.

"But I ain't got your skills."

"I ain't gonna be mad about it, Bolo. Hit it, bro."

Legit he didn't have the technical ability, but he was about size and didn't give a shit about who he walked over. Mikey threw up a big horned heart with a spiked tail and twin pitchforks 🗡, 360° of Knowledge in a six-pointed star, each tip tagged L-L-L-K-W-U, Love-Life-Loyalty-Knowledge-Wisdom-and-Understanding ✡, King David, King Hoover, King Shorty, and B-G-D & S-C-R Nation with a three-slash cross ✞ and then an upside-down crown 👑, cracked five-pointed star ✯, and People ✯ the same direction, along with K-K, UK-K, GL-K, VL-K, and ID-K right side up over an ancient Old English R spray-painted in faded pale blue who knows when. This had always been Royal territory. He stepped back to admire his work for a bit, then threw me the marker and said, "Get it, Midget."

Top popped, I took a huge hit off the Sanford, got to work. Best smell ever, after the naphtha that goes into Zippo lighters, which is right in front of fresh newspaper.

I drew a big Old English S-C-R and N-S-G with a three-dimensional Royal cross ✞, two diagonal slashes and a circle at the top, a bent right ear mad eye cigarette-smoking Playboy Bunny with cross earring in a top hat and bow tie 🐰, an upside-down pyramid with cracked five-pointed star and crescent ☪ finished off with an upside-down playing card suicide King and salutes from us and our sets: COMPLIMENTS OF BOLO AND MIDGET, T/R TOUHY & RIDGE—F/C FARWELL AND CLARK.

Mikey beamed. "That's what I'm talking about."

"Same, homes," I said. "Nice job."

Rusted wheels squealed on burnished steel rails in the distance as we grinned at each other and our work, 98 percent humidity and years of leaked motor oil fuming in the space between us in the packed dirt alley. No one heard us and no one saw us, everyone in the neighborhood at work or lying on the couch watching TV, unable or incapable of giving a shit; the signs and symbols we put up meant nothing to them anyway, as long as the opposition didn't try to burn down the buildings they were tagged on. And it was our job to make sure that didn't happen, even if these folks never knew we were hard at work, every damn day, and doing double time at night.

All that hard work was probably gonna double at least, I thought, after today. Seemed we were going to get details on just how much more we'd have to do for this new Nation, sure, but it felt like there'd be more to it than that, like this was a . . . *portentous* day, kinda like graduation. Things would shift, get really real, maybe more than some folks could handle. We were moving into new areas, with new rules. We never had much use for the old ones other than those that kept us together and in line among ourselves. That had always been enough. Learning a pile of new rules to keep us in line with a bunch of other bangers, well, we'd see if it seemed worth it. Either way, though, I had the feeling things would never be the same again.

The greasy dirt and decayed blacktop alley ended at what we called the cinder path. Five feet wide or so, it ran for a block from Chase to Touhy along the Northwestern tracks and was made up of flint and lava rock chips, hedged in on all sides by dense vines and brambles. This was the way we'd usually start out heading to points south from our neighborhood. The tracks were a whole different world, a deep patch of nature full of trees and vines and tall grass about thirty hilly yards wide on either side of three sets of elevated rails. Today smelled like it did every now and then up by my grandma's house in Michigan when we'd visit in the summer, out in a field where some white guy had poached a deer and took the parts he wanted, left the rest to rot. I stepped about five feet off the path and sure enough there was a slat-ribbed raccoon who looked like he just missed cutting in front of one of the diesel trains that expressed through here on the way to some cushy Highland Park or Lake Forest stop, his little back legs broken and twisted in cruel angles. I leaned in, wanting to put down some tobacco for him or whatever I was supposed to do.

"Leave it, Midget," Mikey said, eyes front, whacking at the tall grass and overhanging leaves with a five-foot deadfall hickory stick he'd probably keep all day now.

"Yeah, yeah, Folks." I hopped back onto the path, threw a whole Newport into the bushes.

Sometimes we'd walk up the grassy embankment onto the commuter line tracks, make our entire way south on the flint rocks and rails. We could also take Ravenswood Avenue, which follows along the tracks on the other side. It was all our turf, so the choice was ours. We decided on street level, cut diagonal from the outlet at Touhy Avenue across a parking lot I'd never seen a single car in, turned right on Clark Street and made a beeline for Farwell Avenue, the other street that makes up the Farwell and Clark branch of Royals. The important parts of the corner itself consisted of Silver Sue's Arcade and my personal favorite, a branch of the Chicago Public Library, along with a pay phone whose number we all knew by heart, 761-5373.

Mikey and I were meeting up at F/C with the set. For Royals, sets consisted of Seniors, Juniors, and sometimes Peewees, just like most other clubs in the city. The Popes had an even younger group called Futures, but that never caught on with us, and neither did the Popes at that time, really, even though some of their seniors tried to recruit us for a minute. The older senior Royals had been united with them back in the day in the UFO ᵁꜰᴅ, along with the TJOs ℑ, Gaylords ✠, and Howard Street Greasers ✝, but that shit got all fucked up and the only sets that stuck together for a while were the Royals and the Popes, and we were still cool with them.

When we got there, everyone was already hanging out, so they were taking it serious, too. Cool. Junior, Mikey2 and 3, Pepper, Miguel, Walter, Slim, RJ, Lil Capone, Hector, a couple of Popes from out by Mather High School tryna club-hop to Royals, and a few of the Peewees new and older, everyone smoking cigarettes, drinking quarts of Old Style, and laughing, but I sniffed out a thin nervous edge to all of it. That was good. These motherfuckers should worry some.

Mikey3

What the fuck am I doing? This shit is nuts. Yeah, it was fine to hang out, get high, drink beers and all, but this is serious. These dudes are crooks. I have a pretty good life. My ma's a waitress who drinks too much, but she remarried, and even though my stepdad is kind of a dickhead, I'm not about this life. I don't need to rebel, get mixed up in some shit I'll never get out of, but you know once you go along with the crowd, it's not easy to walk the other way. There's no way to save face. You have to do the thing. Maybe after you can drift into the background, but in the moment, and this was one of those, you better be all in, show no fear. If I make it through, I'll remember this day for the rest of my life, I'm sure. My life will be nothing like what these guys are facing, the road or two open to them isn't mine, but I can still feel it for a moment. Today is a day of unease, and weight. I pray a little, ask to keep my hands in my pockets and my head down.

Teddy

It occurred to me maybe some of the wannabes, folks not yet initiated in, maybe never wouldbes, should come along, that numbers would make us look good, but in the end, I went with quality over quantity, told the fellas this was gonna be it. I mean for real, what if we got moved on? And the call was skins only, no weapons. These auxiliary cats weren't ready for that shit. Fuck, C/P/W even sent us a couple rolls of tokens for the train so we wouldn't have an excuse to miss it. This was the real shit. We had to treat it that way.

"Henry. What's up, Folks?" The F/C warlord was the first to greet me. Walter and Miguel, their other leaders, were a little ways off, talking quietly together. Henry was the set's warlord. He didn't like his nickname, Slim. He couldn't get rid of it, but it didn't mean I had to use it. We worked together on some things for the set. More and more of them seemed, lately. Today was one of those things, for sure.

"You see it, brother." We shook hands, Royal-style. That's as physical as it gets. This was the '70s. Ain't no motherfuckers hugging each other back then, no sir.

"Y'all ready for this nonsense?" I asked.

"I imagine. Don't matter no way. We're going, ain't it?" He sniffed big and loud. Sort of a tic of his—he always sounded like he had a head cold, but who knows.

"We are. Yes, we are. Hey, brother—you got a Newport?" I reached in my pocket, pulled out my lighter.

"You got them tokens, Teddy?" he asked, handing me a smoke from his pack, taking one for himself.

"I do, Henry. I do. All your boys got a little cash, an address picked out, skins only and no weapons?" I lit my cigarette, kept the flame going for him.

"Can't say for sure on the weapons, homes. I told 'em skins only. But you know how folks act." He leaned in, lit up.

Miguel was the president in this set. He was a Miguel, never a Mikey. His younger brother, Walter, was the vice—a light-skinned dude but a seriously down motherfucker. He was super quiet, so kinda scary, like lots of quiet folks.

WALTER

Man, I've known Teddy for years. He has that thing, you know. I don't know how he does it, but he can talk his way out of any kind of shit that goes down. I hadn't seen him get tagged since his initiation. Maybe 'cause he doesn't have a pretty face, he aims to keep what he has in good shape. Whatever it is, he's good at it. And since his set pretty much folded and he started hanging out here, we got like two warlords now. He still reps for T/R, though, and that's cool, too.

We play foosball together, do tournaments and shit. We're both short, don't look like much, and dudes are always betting against us, but we always win. I play goalie and he's the forward. Has sweet moves and his bank shot from center on the middle three never misses. I can shoot hard enough from my goalie on a pull shot to make it pop out the other side and I do, just to show off. Pretty cool.

This shit he set us up for today was crazy, though. That motherfucker has ideas about what we could do, should do. It's wild, talking 'bout running the whole neighborhood, how we can pay off the cops, run our business on Clark Street out in the open, expand into all kinds of other shit, like girls and cocaine and whatnot, crazy. And yeah, he gets that look in his eyes and all these mugs are "Alright, Folks, let's do it!" and all. He walks out on this wire, takes the rest of us with him. It's crazy how folks go along with it, know what I'm sayin'?

TEDDY

Twenty of us shirtless or bleach white dago T'd, blue or black baggied, black high-topped and suede-rocker shoed, stick-and-poked skin crawling with top-hatted Playboy Bunnies and crosses and Old English Rs, upside-down crowned and bannered nicknames marched east on Farwell for the El at Morse. We took up most of the block walking to the all-stop station where we could grab the first train south to transfer to the Ravenswood line. I drifted to the back of the bunch, looked at the way folks were walking, trying to figure out if anyone's packed, walking hurt or scared. I thought we were in good shape. I floated back up to the front to see where folks wanted to switch trains. We talked about we could do it at Belmont, which is PR Stones ☾▲✳ hood, but they're not around all that much anymore, or at the next stop, Fullerton, which is Insane Unknowns ◈ territory. My preference was Fullerton, 'cause I don't give a fuck and if we ran into some IUKs. Fuck them. It would be a nice warm-up and a sweet start to the day to fuck up some Unknowns. I lived down that way for a while and there weren't too many chances where there were more than two or three of us. Today this mob could put some serious hurt on those jagoffs. I was for real about it, but I got voted down. That's cool. I'd save my energy for the big meeting. I drifted back a couple of rows, lit a smoke, and strolled along. Sometimes democracy is a good thing, I guess, but there's still Fate, ya know? If you pray hard enough, that is.

We rounded the corner from Ashland onto Morse just as a set of those new silver train cars flashed into the station, crispy red, white, and blue stripes snapping, brakes wailing, the crackly voice on the intercom barely audible in the warm breeze starting to kick up off the lake, misted scent of dead alewives and bus diesel twisting in the shimmer off the blacktop in the viaduct below.

"Fuck, bro. We're gonna miss it," Lil Demon said.

"No sweat, Folks. There'll be another one in five minutes," I said.

"What time is it, innyway?" he asked.

"It's not even noon, bro. We don't have to be there till like three or some. It's fine." Mikey popped in from behind.

I watched Demon's peewee face chew the inside of its bottom lip, work out time, distance, and whatever else went on in there. He couldn't read, and math, well, shiiit.

"It's all good, Folks. We got plenty of time," I interrupted his labors.

"Yeah? What if we got too much time?" He up-nodded, chin out.

"So what. We'll chill and visit and whatnot."

"But we don't know any of those guys over there, not really."

He seemed a little spleeny to me, and it took me a minute to figure out why.

Your boy was still pissed because we voted him down on bringing the boom box earlier. That battery-sucking JVC with bass boost was his thing, his anchor. But there was no way we could lug it with us.

It hadn't gone well.

I'd told him, "Leave that shit with Lynette, homes. We can't bring a big ol' box with us, man. It'll slow us down. What if we have to hustle the fuck outta there? You wanna haul a fifteen-pound brick with you trying to cut down alleys and through yards you ain't never been in before? Shit ain't gonna fly, Folks, even if we're doing it to a cool soundtrack."

And he was still mad about it.

A strip of dirty white surgical tape stomped across Lil Demon's nose, each raggedy end underlining a pair of seriously black eyes framing its newly broken state. Last week's initiation by the T/R and C/W Seniors had cratered the middle of his face. It was coming back together, but he still looked like an escapee from an experimental surgery ward. The initiation seemed kind of harsh, and now that I thought about it, all those older cats were whiteboys except for Rabbit, who was Native, Cherokee from down south, and Orlando, who was Black. I wondered if the white dudes went so hard on Lil Demon because he was Puerto Rican, then decided it was better to save those thoughts for later. We had shit to do today. But Lil Demon wasn't letting it progress.

"Come on, Midget. You know you wanted to have tunes." He picked a little more.

"I did. I do. Always will. But this ain't the time for that. You gotta let it go." I'd been losing patience.

Mikey had stepped up and flicked the end of his shattered nose. Lil Demon's eyes welled up, but he didn't cry.

"Your warlord is telling you to leave it, Folks." He pounded the butt end of his hickory stick into the pavement. "So leave it," he said.

Lil Demon left it.

Lil Demon

After I five-ironed that King on Clark Street over by the police station they made me go to therapy, starting when I was locked up at St. Charles. I still had to go, or they'd revoke my parole. Man, seems like I'm going to be on that or probation the rest of my life. I sit in the psychiatrist's office, though, tell him shit he prolly goes home and gets off on. At least it seems that way in our sessions. Some of it is shit I did and some of it is shit I made up. He doesn't care and neither do I. It's what he wants to hear, and it's what I want to tell. We all tell stories that keep us sane, don't we?

Getting initiated in the Royals was harder than I thought. I figured if I jacked some motherfuckers, beat up some Kings, I'd be okay. But it wasn't that easy. Maybe because I'm Puerto Rican these cats are holding the gate closed but it's more than that. Turns out they have standards or some shit. Fuck. It makes me want to join even more.

This shit today is lit. It's so cool, so official-like. It's hard to listen to these cats boss me around and whatnot, but it's their way of making it all work, so I'm gonna be about it. Yeah, fuck people telling you what to do, but if it's for your benefit in the end, you might as well go along with it.

TEDDY

The El stared down at us a half block away. I went to the head of the pack and turned around, walking backward as we passed the little parking lot at the Jewel's, did a quick head count while I pulled my shirt on. We still numbered twenty. Right on. Step one. A five-car off-peak B train shrieked out of the station kitty-corner from us, heading north to Howard Street, end of the line.

"Let's go, Folks. Cross the street and head in." I looked left, right, and left again, cut across Glenwood on the diagonal. The set followed.

The inside of the station in front of the turnstiles and the clerk in the window with the bulletproof glass was now full of Simon City Royals. I admired our assembled selves and pulled out a roll of those tokens a couple of Central Park and Wilson Peewees had brought over. I remembered looking at them on their bikes, thinking about all the enemy territory they'd had to ride through to get to us. Respect.

I snapped off a handful, put the rest of the roll away, then reached into my side pocket and grabbed those Albany Park white pages. I handed the tokens and the book to Henry for the F/C set. "Everyone gets a token, plus pass this around and pick out an address if you haven't already." I smiled, real faint.

"What the fuck, Teddy. You givin' us homework, professor?" Henry laughed.

"I ain't gonna make you do it, but if you don't, and you get busted, they're gonna stick your ass in jail if it looks like you ain't from that hood. Just sayin'. Your call." I raised my left eyebrow, tilted my head, half duck-lipped.

"Shiiiit," he laughed.

"Look at it this way, Folks—you'll have something to read on the ride." I laughed, too.

He didn't smile back. Just turned away, barked at his set to pay attention. They did.

HENRY

Alright, fine. The phone book shit makes sense. Teddy has a pretty good head on his shoulders, is cool to do crimes with and whatnot. He's antsy, always thinking a couple steps ahead like when you play chess, but that's okay, and he's a good lookout 'cause he can see the space around us, but maybe into the future a little bit, too, it seems like. He never disrespects me, always uses my real name, and shushes anyone who thinks about giving me shit about it. Has some kind of vision in the back of his head for how we might be killin' it down the road and I guess anyone who thinks we're gonna outlive the next few weeks is alright by me.

But right now, this professor shit is demanding all my attention. Trying to get these knuckleheads to pick out an address is gonna be a pain in the ass, but they need to do it, I suppose. It makes sense to tell the pigs something, anything, to keep us out of the joint if we get popped in some strange neighborhood. It's gonna be a pile of work to get the whiteboys to play along, but if they do, we'll probably be alright, even if they're the ones who need to the least.

Th nking about them, though, this is gonna be good; their white asses were about to see some brothers from the BGDs and all who *run* shit. Whiteboys are gonna learn something today.

Time to get Folks smartened up.

Lil Capone

Man. How wild. I can't believe I'm going along on this mission or whatever it is. I live in the neighborhood, know a couple of these guys, and then one day I'm helping them beat up some Kings by the Naugle's, so I end up as a Farwell and Clark affiliate. I never got jumped in, never paid dues, only hung out every now and again, but they're cool, don't ask any questions except what's my name. I'm Lithuanian, a Lugan like Lil Psycho, but everyone thinks I'm a DP or a bohunk. I don't want to be none of those, so I tell them my family was Italian from up north, name's Lil Capone, and pray to my chosen namesake it'll keep the questions away. They're cool with it.

Dude. I'm going to St. Dismas for high school. Pretty sure only a couple of these cats have made it past eighth grade, but nobody seems to give a shit. Life is good just hanging out, but it seems like things are about to get really real. I suppose today is going to hand me one of those do-or-die moments. I sit outside myself, think about what that's going to look like. I have an objective view of it, remember reading Sartre's *No Exit* in AP English. I feel cold and warm at the same time, hope I'll live through the day to remember it, because it seems like it might help define a lot for me someday. Everyone is super fired up, and I ride the wave, make my peace with whatever might come. Henry is telling us about some homework he has for us. I'm good at school, so my ears perk up at something I might actually be able to contribute. Hey, all I have to do is pick an address out of the phone book and memorize it. I can handle that, see myself as a city worker one day. I say an Our Father and a couple of Hail Mary Full of Graces, imagine the rest of my day.

TEDDY

I'd found out the hard way at least some of these fellas couldn't read, so I was gambling the ones who could, would help the ones who didn't. And I knew I'd be right, 'cause that's what we did; helped each other. We were family, *made* family, family that mattered way more than most of the families we'd been born into. This big venture into neighborhoods most of these guys had never been to was kinda scary for them. We were responsible for folks here. Sure, it was a pain, but it was also an obligation of love, something that really only these brothers asked of us. We were happy to give it, because we'd be happy to get it in return, if and when we ever needed it. I think for a lot of us this is the vision, the thing we hope for; all that we don't have in our home lives, we make happen in our real lives, in the ways we live our days.

A not-so-far-off squeal of rust and thud of heavy cars on rails started to ramp up from a southbound at Touhy or Estes, hit our ears as we marched through the turnstile one after the other. You could live for a year off the buzz in the set as Folks got turned up, milled around the double doors on the other side of the ticket agent booth.

Everyone properly paid for, we trudged up the stairs to the platform.

It was an A train, the Englewood sign above the driver's booth a bold red under the greasy glass. I up-nodded him behind his darkened window as he pulled into the station, imagined his widening eyeballs at this mob of gangbangers about to get on his train, and tried to look casual and reassuring, imagined he hoped we'd be cool, bring him no grief in his bulletproof cabin, no hassle to his conductor partner.

We settled in, shooting the shit. Folks paired off, cutting each other down, telling jokes, stories of old meetings and older fights, knowing they'd never been to anything like this. I knew for a fact half of these cats had never been south of Wilson Avenue, the stop they got off at to buy baggies and tankers at Z Wallis on Broadway across the street from the El station, the only place around you could get them, and half of them were scared shitless that crazy hillbilly Winthrop and Ainslie or Sunnyside and Magnolia Gay-lords would jump their ass on the way to the store.

I was born in Uptown, down the street from the American Indian Center, and I can testify Uptown was a place you needed to watch your shit. At all times.

There was an all-stops at Loyola coming up, still our territory. Granville was a B station so we wouldn't be pulling in there; then Thorndale, an A-stop, TJO turf, but those cats didn't take the El, were mostly older white dudes with cars; then the Bryn Mawr all-stop, kinda neutral; Argyle in little Chinatown, nothing there; Wilson all-stop, where maybe we'd hook up with Kenmore and Leland Royals from Uptown heading to the meeting, good Folks, mostly hillbilly cats—word was out we were heading their way, so if they were peeking in the cars and waiting smart they'd see us and ride along; then Sheridan, nothing there; blow past Addison, a B-stop with all those Latin Eagles ; and then Belmont with the aforementioned mostly nonexistent PR Stones, where we'd switch to the Ravenswood line even if I wanted to go all the way to Ful-lerton, the next stop. We were gonna be alright. I took a window seat in the first crosswise double row next to the triple seat that ran parallel to the exit doors. Henry perched on the seat next to me, sat diagonal out into the row and kept an eye on his crew.

I chewed the inside corner of my mouth while I looked out the window. There wasn't much to see as we ran along Glenwood Avenue, and I'd been this way on the train hundreds of times, walked it even more; it was mostly apartment buildings and whatnot, occasional shots of our murals big and bold on walls along buildings that cops never really patrolled until later in the '80s when coke started hitting the neighborhood hard. There were a couple of Irish bars that took donations for the IRA, but other than that, meh, though I saw a building where I'd learn how to cook freebase a few years later, so there was that. It was right before the terrain turned sticky and dank, where down on the ground the alleys got confusing, residential and hostile all in the same moment, where TJOs and Kings suddenly appeared, and you had to be on top of your game.

After that it got familiar though unknown pretty quick, I think the books call it unheimlich or something. Like the buildings and alleys looked just like the ones in our neighborhood, but we *knew* it wasn't our neighborhood, that different lives and spirits lived in those spaces, similar but as alien as anything from another world, folks who looked like us, and talked like us, but hated us for who we were. And we hated them right back, even if the reasons why were lost lots of the time, on accident or on purpose, it didn't matter in the end. Anyway, it was reassuring and unsettling at the same time, like you knew it but couldn't know it, could be in it but not from it, a space you should know but wouldn't, couldn't, one this close, but a million miles away. Probably not how most folks see the neighborhood called Edgewater, all casual, but it's forever freaked me out, left me unmoored and unsettled even just taking the bus or the El through it, let alone walking in it. Or talking about it, like right now. It has wild sounding streets like Catalpa. I had to look that one up. Dang. A medicine tree . . . And

Sean High School, a mortal enemy that includes anyone who went there. I can tolerate exactly none of it—the whole show lives in my memory like a tumor I need to have cut out.

Once we cleared that nonsense, got past Foster Avenue and all, things changed for the better. I knew this because as I looked out the window down into the alley in the weird stretch between Ainslie and Lawrence, I watched one red and one brown coyote tear the shit out of a pigeon midmorning, without a care in the world. At first, I thought they had a lapdog between them, a Maltese or something, but it seemed they'd been worrying a huge white cock, a big-breasted snowy male, for so long its ruff and breast feathers had curled and fluffed. That they had no concerns about their activities, ignored the restaurant workers moving in and out with flattened cardboard from early deliveries, gave me a sense of strength and pride I didn't know I needed but was suddenly overjoyed to have. The reddish one lifted his face up to me through the morning haze and winked. It wasn't the first time a coyote had winked at me. I lived walking distance (okay, waaaaalking distance) from the world's greatest free menagerie, the Lincoln Park Zoo. And because it was free, and I could go whenever I wanted, and maybe set some of the piglets free and whatnot, I would visit Mike the Raven, who would say "Hello, Mike" in his cage, which I thought that was a pretty stupid thing to teach a bird, and then after a few visits I figured out it was a *raven,* so of course why wouldn't that be the thing he said over and over all day, irritating the crap out of everyone who gawked by his prison.

Yeah. Lincoln Park Zoo had coyotes living on both sides of the fence, kinda like pheasants on put-and-take hunting farms where the roosters get away but always come back to visit the hens and sit on top of their cages talking shit. The coyotes were like that. I visited them, and the wolves and the buffalo. Seemed like the least I could do, try to be a good relative somehow. Those coyotes, though, yeah, they winked at me, told me stories every now and then. I couldn't understand yet, Sungmanitu Akicita teachings, but they talked to each other, night and day; I could hear them outside our shitty little apartment window when I leaned out to smoke cigarettes and watch the night play out on the street. The local news channels would spotlight a picture some elderly viewer had sent in back when you had to take your film to get developed, when taking pictures was a big deal, an investment. I liked those stories that would show up at the end of the show, during the "human interest" segment to close out the day. *You all have no fucking idea just how human, do you?* I'd ask our little black-and-white Zenith with tinfoil on the antenna.

I smiled big into the even bigger window and turned to look around the car.

RJ was wearing those dark blue cargo baggies we all hesitated to get, the ones with the pale blue stitching—dark and light blue were Taylor Street Jouster colors—but on him no shame, because anyway both his cargo pockets were full of black and royal blue capped magnums. These train cars were gonna suffer, I thought, and that Belmont Avenue stop was gonna look *nice.* Those long-absent Puerto Rican Stones were gonna show up one day headed to a wedding or some shit in the old neighborhood and say *what the fuck?*

This ride is dragging a bit, so I walk to the far end of the car and tag the shit out of the Newport ad up in the corner. Some dude and a chick are smoking cigs in the picture, and it says ES EL SABOR over their heads. I change that shit to ES EL ROYALS HOOD and admire my work. I move back to the El map of all the routes and start fixing that one, too, with some finer print.

I ain't sure about this big meetup. Could be okay, I suppose, or could be a mess of bullshit. Probably we'll take all the grief while the higher-up cats make money off the whole deal. That's how it usually works, how the world works, but maybe this time will be different. I'm not too confident about that last part, but maybe, yeah. Teddy seems to be about it, and I know he thinks about this kind of stuff. A lot. So, there's that.

Really, all I want to do is fuck up the opposition. Maybe we'll get moved on out there, give us a chance to light up some Gaylords or something—there's a branch at Lawndale and Altgeld nearby. It's mostly whiteboys out that way anyhow, so how can we miss? If it's not GLs, it'll be some Freaks or Jousters 🕷 or C-Note$, so fuck it. Same shit, different bucket.

TEDDY

"Hey, RJ. What you doing, Folks?" I said, loud enough to make him jump. He was tagging the citywide CTA map over the exit doors in detail, scratching out the names of stops and writing in ROYALS HOOD over each one.

"You see it, Folks," he said, stepping back to appreciate his work.

Leaning out from my seat to the left gave me a good look. "Nice job," I said.

"Thanks, homes," he said, snap-capping a Sanford blue marker with the palm of his hand. I savored the memory scent as he faced me in the aisle between the exits, swaying in perfect balance with the train. We were hauling ass, the city flying by. His eyes tracked every feature.

"I'm going out between the doors," he said, "gonna have a smoke."

"I'll go with you."

I liked spending time with RJ. School was never his thing; like most of the set, eighth grade was plenty of school for him. Now I thought about it, I was the only core one of us still in school, just passed my second try at freshman year after taking a year off. But RJ was smart, so smart, like lots of us, just not in the ways appreciated by folks not us. And that was okay, 'cause the things we needed to be smart about were things those people never even considered. For us, they were the things that mattered, kept our folks safe, and alive. The coolest thing about RJ was how his mind sat on idle most of the time, cruised along, unengaged, until it was time to do crimes, to get over, to *win*. Then he was the brother you most wanted next to you.

"How you doin', Folks," I asked as the door shut behind us. We were standing in the howl between train cars, one of us each on the little step over the connector. If you looked down you could wide-eye the rusty steel hitches rolling and screeching together, smell the acrid snap of sparks from a train gearing up to go at least forty miles an hour on the long run past Graceland Cemetery between Wilson and Sheridan.

"I'm good, man," he said over the din, pulling out a pack of Newports, shaking one out for himself, then one for me.

RJ had been around in my life since he was eight or nine years old. Seeing him at fifteen, little pedo-stache and hair that looked like it would recede in a few years, was unsettling. I looked into his furrowed face as he cupped a translucent green Cricket lighter in his hands, lit his smoke, and saw him at twenty-five, thirty, then forty. It was strange, but reassuring, too, 'cause in that moment I knew he'd make it to those ages.

"You need this, Folks?" he asked, offering me the lighter.

"Sure," I lied, took it, lit my smoke, handed it back to him.

"Thanks, Midget," he said, stuck it in his pocket.

"What you thinking about today, RJ?" I asked.

"What do you mean?"

"Like, you feeling good about this? Got any vibes?" I asked.

"Seems alright, Folks," he said. "I want to hear what's in it for us, know what I'm sayin'?"

"What do you mean?"

"Like, yeah cool, we're about the Nation and all, but how is the Nation about us, feel?"

He was right. This was the soldier's point of view. Being Folks was cool and all for the brothers in lockdown and that was for real important, but also out here, we were fixin' to get a whole lot of grief. One half of the city was about to square off with the other half. Our traditional opposition was getting plenty of backup, so it made sense to ask if the same was happening for us.

"Good point, Folks," I said. "We need to make sure these other motherfuckers are gonna have our back. If we're expected to stick up for cats like Imperial ♔ Gangsters and Latin 🦅 Eagles, we've gotta have some reassurance they'll move out on Deuces ⚂♠ and Unknowns ♠ and shit."

"For real, Teddy. I know you hadda clash with Eagles and shit down here sometimes just going to school or coming home, now everything is supposed to be cool? How do you feel about that?" He blew the ash off his smoke. It whipped up and away in the wail.

"Well yeah, Folks. You're right. Gonna be kinda weird to be all 'okay cool what's up, Folks' and whatnot when it's been warfare forever."

"Exactly, homes. I'm having a hard time seeing how it's gonna work, know what I'm sayin'?"

"I do." Shit.

"Yup." He read my face, leaned back against the door, held his right upper arm with his left hand, Folks-style, looked me up and down. It wasn't a challenge, but it was a legitimate question.

We finished our smokes listening to the wind and the rails.

RJ

We'll see. Those big shot motherfuckers'll wanna take the glory and all while we're out here soldiering, reckoning with the bullshit. That's fine, den. Teddy can talk to them and all, keep it real, but we're gonna need to get paid, too. These cats making deals and whatnot, protecting our brothers in the joint, yeah, that's cool, but also shit like the Christiana and Wellington set coasting off that National Guard rip-off with the AR-15s they did—what have you done for the Nation lately? It's all good, I suppose, but motherfuckers need to put in some work, feel? Whatever. That negotiation shit is beyond me, but I trust Teddy and Henry. They'll look out for us. They both look out for me, all the time.

That's enough of that. Shit's exhausting, bro, know what I'm saying? You gotta save that kind of brain power for other stuff. Right now, I'm peeping these neighborhoods for jobs. Gonna have to come back down this way on off days. Shit's looking juicy as hell.

TEDDY

We had a ways to go until Sheridan, never mind the Belmont stop, and some folks were looking edgy. Some of them were mooning over at the big long cemetery running by the west-facing windows. I was standing near the door between cars, assessing the situation when RJ said, "Hey Teddy. Tell us a story."

Shiiit, I thought. "'Bout what, homes?"

"I don't care," RJ said. "But make it about school, though. I fuckin' hate school."

"Okay. What else? Someone give me a name for the teacher. Who did you dirty? Anyone? Y'all got a teacher you hate?"

Mikey said, "Mrs. Bame. Remember her? We used to smoke cigarettes in the back of her class. Hash even a couple times." He laughed, said, "She looked like a bird. Like a pigeon."

"Like Mrs. Peacock from Clue," Henry said.

"Who?" RJ and Mikey said.

"Never mind, Folks," Henry said. "Yeah. Like a pigeon."

Fuckin' Pepper, ulp ulp hee haw, said, "Make it about someone from our Nation. Like a HSG or something." Pepper used to tell folks he was a Howard Street Greaser. But he wasn't. I knew those cats. Half of them cried when Elvis died and they didn't know Pepper at all, even if he tattooed a shitty little HSG with a four-pointed cross on his fat, splotchy arm.

"But with some mayhem and shit." Lil Demon grinned.

"And maybe a little bit funny, too, Teddy," Hector threw in.

Jesus Christ. I breathed deep, said,

Blond hair parted down the middle, teeth seriously bucked, six mustache hairs and cheeks on fire with zits, he shouted Gaylord Killer! last night right before he puked on sad, sad Angela, his three-months-pregnant girlfriend.

Her ma just cried at their kitchen sink, two blocks away in a sweaty, cramped three-flat on the corner of Lawrence and Francisco as Angela's cat pissed on top of the Cubs hat he left on her back porch bedroom floor that afternoon.

His name was Gale. Its boy-girl nature made him angrier by the day. His children will suffer for it.

And so will his innocent liver.

Even with the stigma of the lady name, Gale was pretty popular with the chicks. He's a good kisser but won't tell how he got that way. You could ask his cousin Leah, with

*whom he's drunk plenty bottles of Boone's Farm at fam-
ily gatherings, but the last time she talked about it, Gale
blacked her eye at Cousin Tommy's wedding reception,
then turned and put out his Kool 100 in the mostaccioli.
Gale and his too-dark blue eyes can be warm, sure, but
when he's cold, yeah. The iceman cometh, as long as he can
keep Billy Squier in the background.*

*And right now, he couldn't shake the image of Squi-
er's tight pants poster on the back of his bedroom door.
His mouth silently twisted with rage in the back of the
Carl Schurz High School freshman English class he's now
attempting for the third time. He picked at something
on his left cheek, tap-tap-tapped his pencil with his right
hand on the shitty old desk full of Gaylord graffiti. He
snapped the No. 2 in half, stuffed the ends down in the
out-of-date hole that used to be for an inkpot back in the
day. He reached into his pocket, pulled out an antique
Barlow Jack Knife that his dad gave him one drunken
afternoon, snicked it open, and carved "Insane ♥ Popes"
into the maple desktop, thoughtfully brushing the wood
chips onto the floor. Finished, he started to gouge Angela's
name into his left forearm, got to the "g" and went too
deep on the little foot part, blood seriously leaked onto
the desk. Fuck. He can't even do this right. He slapped
both hands down in front of him, hard. The whole class
flinched.*

*Mrs. Bame felt his hatred and shame collect with thirty
years of other angry-little-shit students and burn its way
into her heart and to the head of her classroom on the
decrepit building's fourth floor. Retirement's a too-far five
years down the road. She couldn't take it anymore. She
walked away from her desk and over to one of the huge*

low-slung antique windows for some fresh air. Her wither-
ing hands brushed away flaking cream lead paint and she
opened the sash wide, jumped.

Gale pocketed his knife while most of the other students
ran to the sun-washed bank of windows, stared down,
hands over mouths, heads shaking. He wondered what
Angela was doing right now, lit a smoke.

Fuck it. There's no teacher here, right?

"You whom'd it, you fucker! Nice!" Mikey said. A couple bored
old folks shuffled past onto the platform at the last second.

"Good one, Teddy," RJ said, the doors whooshing shut. "Fuck
those Popes, anyway."

Lil Demon was looking out the big window on the east side
of the car as we pulled out of the Sheridan stop, deciphering the
murals and tags on the backs of buildings in a neighborhood he's
never seen before, grinning.

Then I heard a big laugh erupt from Hector. He was holding
on to the pole by the exit door, doubled over, slapping his knee.
Hector is the set's enforcer. He's like four foot six but works out
twice a day so he's seriously jacked. He has a brother who could
be his twin except he's a couplethree years older, Lil Bugs. I think
they're Irish or something, lots of babies and little ones here and
there, some you remember, a Cullen or Keenan, some you never
see again. "Gale," Hector said, gulping air.

"Wait. What's up with Gale?" Pepper squinted. Henry, Mikey,
and RJ just laughed, and we rolled down the line for a while.

Back in my seat I looked out the window at Wrigley Field whipping by. In ten years, it would slide into total yuppie–Big Ten
asshole central. For now, it was still Ernie Banks's parking lot,
a donut shop, and tons of Latin Eagles. They were a pain in the

ass, yeah, but up on the far north end of the platform they had cut a hole in the heavyweight diamond grate put up by the CTA to fence people out so you could sneak onto the platform if you dared their back porches and stairwells. Most days it was worth it; the old man gave me a dollar a day for school so if I could save the thirty-five-cent fare in the morning, I could have lunch or most of the price of a pack of smokes. If I overspent, I'd have to sneak on at the Jarvis stop by putting my back against the utility pole and walking eighteen feet up the wall and hopping over the third rail to the platform. All that nonsense is probably why I went into . . . business, at fifteen. And yeah, while we're on contradictions or questions, even though I'm a stone North Sider I'm a White Sox fan. Have been since I played in a Little League All-Star game at Comiskey Park back in '77, so don't give me any shit.

I pulled out my copy of *Boss,* turned to my favorite passage, the one that talked about how Old Man Daley figured out he could round up votes for himself instead of the precinct captain, took his South Side Back of the Yards gangbangers to the top, took all of Bridgeport, then became the mayor, the ultimate club president and dream. I don't admire too many people, but the man who had our schools and the city flying the world's best metropolitan flag at half-mast for two weeks and got us the day off for his funeral was one of them. I got a thing for alternate governments, be they Roma, Italian, or Irish, or whoever will step into the breach, take care of order and adjudication where the over-culture won't, where the government that serves the whites of the world doesn't give a shit about the rest of us. They crab and complain about how Cosa Nostra costs us extra in payola and bribes, but you know what, you all collect taxes for shit that helps exactly none of us, so who gives a fuck. At least on the South Side the fireworks paper gets swept up after the Fourth of July and folks who have a problem in the neighborhood can go see someone who'll listen to them.

The train pulled into the station at Belmont in dramatic ways. Our driver was going full speed until the last possible moment, showing off for folks who'd never see it; he hit the brakes so hard I watched the spirit blue sparks arc and laugh across the third rail and wink out against the wooden-planked platform. I half stood in my seat, looked up and down the car, counted off a quick twenty. We were all still here, would always be here, I guessed.

"Let's go, Folks," I said. T/R folks and the rest of my crew got up.

Henry stood, swept his hands forward. F/C groaned and pulled out of their seats.

We made our way toward the exit doors. Everyone filed out together. Not gonna lie, Folks, it gave me shivers to see our set moving in such large numbers.

Getting off the train, I motioned for everyone to follow me. We needed to cross over the tracks on the pedestrian bridge to the other platform. Twenty Royals trudged up the stairs and then yes!

who do we meet halfway across

but

Lil Ghost, Sir Knight, Bashful, and Young Lover from the Halsted and Wrightwood Unknowns ♠. Black Chuck Taylors with black laces. Black baggies and T-shirts. Their set was all mixed, too—they looked like us, but definitely *weren't* us.

Not gonna lie. I was *so* excited. These motherfuckers. What a gift. Even though I got voted down on getting off at Fullerton, here they were at Belmont, Coyote or someone good looking out.

"What's up, Peoples." RJ stepped to these bitches instantly.

"Ain't nothin, Folks. Just passin' through," Sir Knight said.

"You sure about that, Peoples?" Mikey said.

"Yeah," Lil Demon said. "You probably ain't passing through. Not like you think."

"It's cool, Folks," Sir Knight offered.

"Oh no it ain't." I showed him my teeth, top and bottom.

"Teddy?" Mikey asked.

"Oh, it ain't, Folks," I confirmed.

Hector strolled up, said, "Cool, Folks," and smashed his left forearm into Sir Knight's chest, grabbed up his shirt, reached down behind his knees and heaved his top two-thirds over the side of the walkway. "Is it cool now, Peoples?" He held on to Sir Knight's legs, dangled him over the electrified tracks about fifteen feet below. I looked over the top of my shades to see an Evanston Express howl through Diversey station heading our way.

For real, Sir Knight let out some screams I remember to this day.

Lil Demon laughed in a way I'll never forget, either. My set had some sociopaths that could redefine case studies. We all carried some baggage but holy crap, for real, a few of these cats had some deep shit happened to them. The world paid for it. Would keep on paying for it.

Lil Demon

Hahaha. I got this therapist while I'm on probation who won't look me in the eye. Tells me on our first day that he's heard it all, I couldn't scare him, my shit was just petty and whatnot. I laid some Boricua shit on him he couldn't handle, then poured it on about the home abuse. One day I tell him about scalping this King and he's all *nah,* and then he tries to excuse himself and I'm like, "Wait, let me tell you how it makes me feel," and after I yell at him about how good it is he gets me assigned to some chick who is a week out of school, but I feel bad and just tell her that I have some family problems and we talk about the weather or whatever. His name is first on the door but he's the last in my book, the fucking pussy. Where do they find these guys?

TEDDY

Hector pressed his forearms against Sir Knight's legs, holding him in place, then leaned over and bunched his shirt up with both hands, yanked him back onto the platform. While Knight stared down with awe at his feet back on solid ground, Hector buried his left fist in his gut and knocked him out with a right hook to his temple. Sir Knight crumpled in a heap on the bridge.

Out of nowhere, Henry popped in with his big fat fist thrown deep from the shoulder and tagged Young Lover in the forehead. His pretty ass went down like you do with one of those hits.

"Man, fuck these punks, Teddy." He offered one of those grins.

"Right on, brother." I returned it.

Lil Demon ran up on the other two Unknowns who had retreated to the top of the stairs they'd just climbed and kicked Lil Ghost dead in the chest. He went ass over teakettle all the way down the steps, clocked his head against one of the dividers on the platform. He wasn't moving.

Young Lover looked at his fallen bros, raw fear on fire in his eyes.

"Get him, Hector." I up-nodded.

Hector caught Young Lover halfway down the stairs and threw him over the railing down onto the tracks.

Holy fuck.

He landed on his back on the wood-planked utility platform off to the side of the third rail.

RJ laughed.

Jesus Christ. I shook my head.

Young Lover stooped across the tracks, skipped the third rail, and hauled himself up onto the platform we'd just come from.

"Missed one," Hector said.

"It's alright, bro," I said. "He won't forget that shit for a while."

"Still, bro. I missed."

"It's okay, brother," I said, thinking yeah, we dodged a murder 1 bullet for sure.

These Unknowns were in disarray like I'd always dreamed of, always hoped for whenever I had to slink by them on Broadway and Diversey in my own neighborhood. No one had died, sure, but still, they were living in a fear they'd never known. That might've been better, actually.

HECTOR

I for real would drop this UK over the side of the bridge, but yeah, probably better to keep it clean since we're on our way to the big meetup. Still. Wish I could've.

Anyway, it's good to put hands on someone new. I don't know these Unknown motherfuckers at all, but Teddy does, and he really seems to hate them for his own reasons. I don't give a fuck; opposition is opposition. Same shit different bucket to me. You need some Peoples or whatever fucked up, I'm your man.

It's a good start to what feels like a great day coming on. It's nice to get out of the neighborhood, go on an adventure and whatnot. I never really got down this way too much, except that one time we had to take my baby brother to an appointment at Children's Hospital. We went there together on the El, came home in a cab without him. That was a shit day.

TEDDY

The Ravenswood train we needed was screeching into the station, so we hustled down the stairs. Lil Ghost was still laid out on the planks. Mikey kicked him in the face as we passed by. A gang of bluehairs clutched their purses and Ann Sather's doggy bags tighter and were suddenly deeply interested in anything happening on the other side of the platform. Their eyes rolled like the pigeons who flew up in anger at a train's first approach. I tried to smile reassuringly but it landed flat in light of the recent . . . incident up top, and they pretended not to see me. I waved anyway and herded folks into the nearest car, counting heads as I went, thinking about the fat Swedish cinnamon rolls they were probably bringing home to their sad-sack husbands.

Everyone made it safe, and we owned an entire car on the Ravenswood line. The two or three passengers reading newspapers and chitchatting about the headlines had discreetly fucked off to other cars as soon as we started piling in. Now RJ was walking around, busy tagging anything that'd hold color. Mikey had a double seat to himself, so I figured I'd check in with him, see what he thought of my ideas for getting us to the meeting nice and safe. He was hunched forward laughing softly, slowly shaking his head, left arm cradling his stick, right hand rubbing the top of his head. I sat down across from him, turned in the row of seats next to the door, showed my top teeth and said softly:

"Here's the plan, Folks. Half of us are getting off at the Kedzie stop with Hector and the other half are getting off with me at Kimball, the end of the line. And we're gonna walk back from there."

"How are you gonna pick, Folks?" Mikey asked, head slightly nodding with the rhythm of the train hauling over the tracks.

"What do you mean?" I said.

"Who's going with who?" he said.

"For real? Who gives a fuck?"

"You do," he said. "I know you. Tsssss." He rubbed the side of his face.

He was right.

"Well," I said, "I figure we'll mix it up, have folks from both sets in each group, show that unity, that strength we got in the set."

"Who's going with you, Teddy?" He stuck out his chin at me.

"You." I up-nodded back.

"Mmm-hmm. Who else?"

"Probably you, Henry. Lil Demon, Junior. Rollo. Miguel, Walter." I crossed my arms, left over right. "RJ and Hector can lead the other set with Pepper and them—they'll be closer to where we're going."

"So, like, they won't get lost?" he said.

"Yeah. Exactly."

"Bullshit," he called, grinned big.

"What?" I scrunched both brows.

"You're trying to play it off like you're helping the not-too-swift set, but for real, Folks, you're segregating."

"Say what?" I looked out at the back porches whipping by. Old ladies were hanging laundry, watering plants. A guy throwing out his trash gave us the finger.

"Yeah, Midget. All those brothers you just named off for the second crew are whiteboys." He laughed.

"Shiiiiit."

"You know it's true, Folks."

Damn it.

"Nah, bro. No way," I weak-protested.

"Oh, yes. Many ways."

"Hunh." I had nothing.

"I ain't trying to tell you how to run your show, man, I'm just sayin'."

"Appreciate that. Do you think anyone'll notice?" I had no plans to change jackshit.

"I don't know. Do you care if they do?" he asked.

"Not really, I guess. Fuck 'em."

He rubbed his hair, laughed. "Yeah. Fuck 'em." He shook his head, looked down at the pile of trash under his seat. "But remember what you did. And own that shit."

RJ

It makes sense that we'd head up in two crews once we got off the train. There are way too many of us to travel that far without getting made or drawing the cops. We'll probably hear in a few how shit's going down. And yeah, I still need to pick out an address from the phone book, so I don't get popped or whatever for not being from the neighborhood. Not sure how that was going to work, but Teddy seems pretty hype to get it right. I'll see what I can do, try to find an easy one to remember.

TEDDY

"A right, y'all. Here's what's good. We're fixin' to split up when we make our way on the last leg to Central Park and Wilson. We're getting off at two different El stops and then walking over to the schoolyard. RJ, Hector, Pepper, Psycho—you and the rest of those folks sitting with you right now get off at Kedzie. I'll tell you how to get to Roosevelt when we're closer to the station." I was standing up, hanging on with both hands to the overhead rail. I scrunched my head low on my shoulders and looked out the window. I stared deep as I could, trying to see the Mississippi way out west or something, anything to look smart and thoughtful. And like I was remembering important shit.

"C/P/W said the cops should be chill, but don't give them any reason to fuck with us," I lied. They'd said no such thing, but I wanted to keep folks from getting jumpy and prone to running. "Keep your heads down and your hands in your pockets. Stick to the sidewalk and head right over to the schoolyard and you'l be alright. No fucking around."

RJ seemed antsy. If he stayed chill, we'd be fine, but sometimes he went off. When he got like this, it was fifty-fifty shit was gonna happen. I reached in my pocket, pulled out a quarter and flipped tails. We were going to be okay for now.

There were a couple of groans from the crew, mostly for looks I guessed, and everyone eased back for the long ride. RJ shot me a look. I took it along with my seat.

RJ

Thinking maybe I got stuck on the dumbass crew, but then I look around close-like. Yup. These are all whiteboys. What the fuck, man, I'm on a whiteboy crew. We'll make it work, but still. When I saw Teddy look at me and flip a coin, I wasn't sure if that was to pick the squad I was gonna be in or if it was for some other crazy shit he had cooking in his brain. I knew he held a grudge against my ma for being a Latin Queen, but he never held it against me personally, and I didn't think he was about to start. Whatever. I'm not gonna worry about it. We'll see what this trip brings.

TEDDY

Boss in hand, I settled in for the long haul out to the Northwest Side. I was looking forward to seeing Roooosevelt High School. Not gonna lie, I was a little excited, even if I kept it to myself. Nelson Algren and Shel Silverstein went to Roosevelt. I'm pretty sure I was the only one who knew that, but whatever. I like books. Fuck you.

I read the Hamburg Athletic Club section again, felt a little sleepy. The train'll do that to you. Shiiit. One time I got on the El at Belmont to go to school for first period, starting at 8:10. It was January or something, colder than death anyway, and I found a seat over the heater. I fell asleep. It happens even if you need to be vigilant as fuck, but I was still at Belmont when I woke up. I was like shit, that was weird, 'cause it was one of those when you fall asleep in the wild and it works, means something, you know, you wake up like damn—I am *refreshed*. So, I knew I had slept for sure but what the fuck, how am I at Belmont still? We were pulling out of the station and there were only a few people on the car. The light in the sky looked off, so I asked this old white-haired dude across the aisle what time it was by doing the pointing to an imaginary watch thing.

He said, "It's a quarter to ten."

Shiiit.

"What?" I said.

"English?" he said.

"What?" I said again.

He goes, "Do you speak English?"

"I do okay," I said.

"Alright then, son. It's a quarter to ten in the morning."

"Thanks."

Holy shit. I had kicked back and crashed out to the end of the line at Howard Street, turned around, went all the way down to Jackson Park at the other end, then back up north again. Hahaha. I checked my pockets right away. I'd seen motherfuckers razor-blade people's pockets and take their shit. Nope. I was all set. Dang. I was toast for school for the day. Since I was on a B train, I figured I'd get off at the next stop, Addison, and go back home. Fuck it. I tried, right? If I hurried, I could get high and catch most of *The*

Price Is Right with my Native homeboy Leksi Bob Barker. There were worse ways to spend the morning.

But now, I got a big day and plenty of shit to juggle in my head. Dreams, if I could remember them, were usually welcome, but they weren't gonna help here so I needed to stay awake. I stuffed the book in my side pocket and looked out the window, tapped some threes, fingers to thumbs, pinkies first. We were heading through better neighborhoods, less graffiti, more houses, nicer porches on the big buildings. I hadn't been on the Ravenswood line too much and wondered who lived in these cribs, took note of the clean apartment houses, places with porches where people stacked their returnables outside their back door. I made a fair profit back in the neighborhood by returning those bottles and keeping the money while their owners were at work, figured I was doing folks a favor, really, 'cause what grown-ass person wants to return a bunch of pop bottles for chump change? I'd be heading out to these new neighborhoods sooner rather than later; shit was ripe for my assistance. Who knew these nice people were contributing to the cinematic education of underprivileged youth? Whenever I went bottle hunting on Fridays it was for money so we could go to the movies that night. I merely engaged their unrealized humanitarian urges, performed my version of civic duty, was being a good neighbor, really. Building community and all.

Kedzie and then Kimball were only a few stops away. The tension was starting to crank up the closer we got. I knew this because the spot that carried it all between my neck and right shoulder blade was on fire. Whenever shit was about to go down, or I was gonna get in trouble, either or both, that spot on my back felt like someone was gouging it with a hot poker. And right now, well, yeah. I could actually feel the heat with my fingers when I reached back and touched it. I was ready and not ready all at the same time.

This was a big moment. And maybe it was just me, but everyone's words were louder, laughter longer, eyes brighter. I made a note to myself to remember that shit.

Those last two stops were both at-grade stations, mostly a rarity on Chicago's elevated and subway lines, and the howl of the cars glanced and echoed off the garages lining the alleyway they snaked through. I had zero concept of real estate markets, but even I knew those houses were probably pretty cheap, like the shitholes that followed the flight paths in Bensenville out by O'Hare. Noise was a marker of poverty and neglect, I was sure.

As we slowed into Kedzie I got up and surveyed the car, one hand hanging on to the pole by the exit door, the conductor hitting the brakes in a rhythm only he could hear, all of us jerking along to his drum.

I pushed my hair off my forehead, said good and loud, "RJ, Hector. Grab up Pepper and them and get off here. Head to the end of the station, take a right on Kedzie to Eastwood then go right again and move out west to the Roosevelt schoolyard. It's at the dead end of the street. You can't miss it. Take a right at the school, then a left on Leland down to Central Park, then another left to Wilson. Heads down, hands out, no fucking around. Get a feel for the neighborhood so you know how to get to the meetup spot in case we have to run. We'll meet you at the schoolyard in a bit."

Pepper had to pop off.

"Why don't we all get off here, Midget?" he gulped, stepping.

"Think about it." I walked over closer so we wouldn't have to yell across the car.

"What?" he asked, challenging a little.

This fuckin' peckerwood.

"Whut?" I mocked in his accent; made like I had big buck-teeth. This motherfucker. He'd always be telling me how his great-grandma or someone was a Cherokee princess. Been hearing that crap my whole life and it's never meant jackshit. Ain't a one of them actually ever been Indian. Man, I'm an enrolled tribal member on my dad's side and my mom's a Johnny Cash Tennessee Injun hillbilly and still got way more Native than he'll ever sniff. But I didn't bother to get into all of that, just said, "Two dozen of us gonna cruise out of here and down the street in broad daylight? How does that look? It's gonna be hard enough with us in two groups. Shiiiiit. You're lucky you're a dumbass. If I thought you were smart enough to make it on your own, I would have had a pile of you get off back at Francisco and walk your asses thirteen blocks to the meeting."

"You ain't gotta get nasty 'bout it," Pepper said.

Man, I hated this redneck fuck and knew I wasn't the only one in the set who did. I knew he'd been gunning for me forever. Folks told me everything. They wanted me to take him out, but I'd been cool about it for a minute. "I ain't being nasty, just truthful, motherfucker," I said.

"Fine, then." He looked down at his feet.

"Fine, den," I said. "Get back with RJ and them and get ready to go."

"Alright, Folks," he offered.

"Alright. Stay up, Folks," I said, a little sorry, patted him once on his Band-Aid-colored shoulder. Some of these white whiteboys had weird-looking skin, even in the summertime, maybe especially then.

He skulked back to the crew. RJ locked eyes with me, laughed a little, up-nodded. Him and Hector hustled up their folks, and that set shuffled over and out the exit. Nervous chatter lifted up, drifted out onto the platform, a ball of energy passing through the closing doors, drowning out the conductor on the PA. I did a quick check. The whiteboys were following the rules. Most of them weren't violating the skins-only decree. I knew without checking a few had knives or chains and whatnot, and it looked like Lil Psycho had a chrome .22 auto in his waistband. That was okay, though. We might need it, and he was pretty levelheaded in certain situations. Still though, I thought about Chekhov from Honors English, shuddered a little.

PEPPER

Fuckin' Injun. Teddy is such a prick. I don't get why he doesn't like me. My great-grandma was a Cherokee princess, but he never seems to care about that, won't even acknowledge it. It doesn't make any sense. His mom was from down south, too, but I think her grandma was Black. He should be kissing my ass, but he can't give me the time of day. I think he thinks I'm dumb or something. But I ain't. I'm just trying to get along, do the right thing, but he makes it hard. Shit. Fucker even told me my beautiful blond girlfriend, Pansy, was ugly one time. Not cool. I always think he'll get what's coming to him. Right now, though, it seems like he's got a whole lot coming to him, all of it good. I don't get it. But we'll see. He's gonna get his. I oughta be the leader of this whole set. And he needs to fuck off somewhere, anywhere else. If it was up to me, he'd get fifty to the chest and sent on his way.

My spot's gonna come up.

TEDDY

The doors closed and the rest of our set was on our way to Kimball, last stop on the Ravenswood line, like it or not. Once we got there, we'd need to make our way to meet up with C/P/W and then head to the schoolyard. We were about two hours ahead of schedule, so that was good. I wanted us in position and with a feel for the area, even if I'd already studied the map. It's one thing to know a place on paper, but it's never any good to be totally out of place with no sense of the turf you're in, with no time to adjust, to look around at the buildings, the back porches, the alleys in the neighborhood. If you can't see an escape route, you're going to be looking for it the whole time you really need it. It's distracting and dangerous.

The train pulled out, squeals from the tracks and squelches from the PA ringing loud, its rusted roots pulling hard on the polished rails, the tang of electric arcs twisting silent smoke up into the ventilation system; it was almost impossible to talk until we got well underway. It gave me a minute to collect my thoughts, think about what I'd say. Even though this shit seemed easy, it was carrying all the world to make it seem effortless. And that pressure was there, always there, the crush to make it seem like you were just talking out your ass, like what you'd said was rolling, flowing in the most natural way. That's how you do. But it took a lot.

I had been holding on to the overhead bar with both hands, looking out the window. Now I turned and grabbed the back of a seat with one hand, stood in the middle of the aisle. I raised my voice, said, "Alright, Folks, end of the line coming up. No worries. This is where we want to be." The car jilted and jilked, right to left and back. We angled with it, rolling along in its caroms and tilts. Everyone faced me.

"It's all good, Folks. We ready?" I asked.

"For sure, Folks," Mikey2 said out of nowhere. He hadn't said a word all day.

"Bet," Henry said.

Lil Demon cheesed big, said, "Oh yeah, Folks. We ready."

That was good enough for me. I couldn't think of a crew I'd rather be with. I sat down in the triple sideways seat by the door, gathered for a storm I hoped wouldn't come.

MikeyZ

I can't get busted, no way. My dad will kill me. He's from Sicily, works his ass off and drinks a lot, fills his own bullets on his workbench down in the basement, but he takes good care of us, makes sure I always have money in my pocket. And will kick my ass if he finds out I'm hanging out with these guys. He's a for real bigot, doesn't like Black or brown people. He tolerates Teddy being around, will grab his hands and look at his tattoos, ask him if he's a pachuco all the time, whatever the fuck that is. Thinks his being Indian is pretty okay. My ma adopted Teddy, Sicilian-style. He's my brother that way and shit is nuts, but still, this is cool. I wouldn't miss this meeting for the world. We have fun in the neighborhood, stealing cars and doing shit like that, but this is kinda big-time, like in the movies, like *The Warriors* or something.

Anyway, this is gonna be it, the last summer for me. The old man is already talking to me about dropping out, going to work. For him it's work, work, work. He doesn't give a rat's ass about school. Man, I'm not sure he ever even went to one now that I think about it. That's fine. School was shit. Teddy goes, says it's nothing but Kings and Vice Lords anyway. Who needs that kinda crap? I have a job lined up for September at the Burger King over on Devon. I'll be outta this neighborhood and making money before too long anyways, so I might as well enjoy myself for now.

TEDDY

We pulled into the station pretty smooth, the conductor probably off after this shift, dreaming about lunch and heading home. I was kinda hungry myself, but it was best to stay that way until after this shit was over. Food makes you dopey, lazy. I'd eat tonight or something. Supper is the best meal, anyway, remember? For now, I had stuff to do, but still, I really wanted to eat at some point.

I stood up.

"We ready?"

"Ready, Folks"—a chorus.

"Alright. Let's do this."

We marched off the train. I listened to the hum of the air system, the idling, emptying cars. A sense of finality echoed over the empty seats; the cars seemed to miss their passengers in palpable ways. Out on the street I saw a Huddle House right there on Kimball. Shiiit. One of my favorite hillbilly restaurants, where the waitresses had tattoos on their hands like we did, called you "hon," and took care of you. I imagined my ma, who was a waitress, too, took care of her customers like that, even if she ignored me, my brother, and my sisters at home. You can't have it all. No time now, though, but maybe on the way home . . .

"Teddy, can we stop at the store?" a voice drifted up.

Jesusfuckinchrist, it was like the road trips I'd take with my kids years later. Any travel more than forty-five minutes and you have to stop for snacks.

"Sure, homes. What do you need?" I threw back. I knew it wasn't anything in particular.

"I don't know. Maybe some chips or some. A pop. You know."

"Yeah, yeah. Fine." This is why I wanted to get here early.

We stopped at the first little convenience store on the way. I bought a box of Marb Reds and a pop. Henry got some Jays Hot Stuff chips.

"Want some?" he asked.

"Thanks, bro." I reached in for a few.

It's kinda wild now, you see Flamin' Hot stuff everywhere, but Jays in Chicago was doing that business back in the day, way before folks at Cheetos got any wise ideas. I think they had the cool-ass lil Hot Stuff Devil 👹 for a mascot, the one who'd end up doing overtime as a symbol for Satan's Disciples. Shiiit, they even made it with popcorn, the O-Ke-Doke. And if we couldn't find Hot Stuff, we'd get regular chips, open them up, dump in a bunch of hot sauce, shake it all up. This is the way.

Henry ate a handful, coughed.

"Fuck, Midget." His eyes watered.

"I hear you, Folks." I twisted the cap off the bottle of Pepsi I had bought, handed it to him. He drank deep, handed it back.

"Thanks, bro," he said.

"Ain't nothin', Folks." I chewed and swallowed my chips, eyes watering, took a big drink myself. We both burped, laughed a little.

I looked up; saw we were almost to Wilson Avenue. Once we hooked west, we'd be on our way over to the main branch and then the meeting, no coming back. I turned around, checked out the crew. I was surprised we hadn't seen any cops at all. Kinda wild, but I wasn't complaining. Everyone was chilling, snacking and talking shit. All good.

We moved with a purpose up Wilson Avenue. I took note of the alleys, counted out some threes on the ends of my fingers, tap-tap-tap, repeated my address, 4703 N. Bernard, to myself. No cops yet, but it was only a matter of time, I figured. My shoulder had quieted down, but still.

"Hey Teddy, do you want this phone book back?" Henry asked.

"Yeah. Let me have that," I said. He handed it over. I took it and walked down the first alley a little ways, threw it in a dumpster.

"I get it," he said, when I came back.

I knew he would. If the cops found that on us, we'd all be fucked. I had it memorized, innyways. I thought about the things I turned my limited brain power to. I wished I spoke Portuguese, or Italian, or even better, Spanish, something that would tell me I was awake and alive, moving beyond all the lines they told me I had to live within.

HENRY

Shit is wild out this way. It's . . . quaint, like my grandma would say. There are tons of trees and whatnot. Probably even have those little city-owned play-lot parks and stuff for kids.

Weird how different it can be. It is what it is, but still, even though these were Polacks and DPs and shit, they're white, so the rules are different. Motherfuckers can come over here and get status right off the bat and the boat, don't have to do nothing but be white. For real it's not *great,* not some Lincoln Park–level business, but still. A little bit like the suburbs, I guess. If it wasn't for the El going by every now and again it could be Skokie or some. Me and my ma and my two brothers have done some immigrating of our own, moved up to Rogers Park when I was a little kid, and now she takes a two-hour ride on the El six days a week back out to the South Side to make potato chips for Jays. We don't see her much, but the lights are always on.

I'm looking forward to what the other sets from across the city have to say, to seeing how this Nation is going to work. It's cool there are some brothers calling the shots and whatnot. Our own neighborhood needs some goals, some direction, a sense that someone has our backs while we are out there. This is a new way for us. It feels like we're about to elevate, and I'm not too sure everyone is down. We'll probably gain some folks, lose even more. RJ usually has some real talk about shit like this. Teddy knows what's up about stuff all the time, shares his pros and cons, but in this instance, he seems super down with everything. I trust him, but still, I want a second opinion at least.

TEDDY

Man, this was an allllright neighborhood. Some decent apartment buildings without graffiti and a few nice houses. Except for the El in the background every five minutes, it was pretty quiet. But the farther we walked, the less we could hear the rails and the brakes from the train yard. It looked like our neighborhood, except cleaner. Wilson was still a two-way street, but it didn't look like the one in Uptown at all.

Lots of trees and shit. Even some little gardens. Nice.

We walked on. I was kinda worried that with no stressors the boys would find something to put in their own way, break some windows, set a dumpster on fire, but they were chilling, enjoying late summer's desperate light and a fine inland breeze. If they were anxious about the upcoming meeting, they didn't show it. Maybe they were appreciating being in a decent neighborhood as much as I was.

Roosevelt went by on our right and even that was in pretty good shape for a place built in the '20s. I looked around at the passageways, backyards. If we had to take off, the clearest paths opened down alleys south away from the school, but the El was east and north. We'd be in no-man's land and then Gaylords and Kings and who knows what. Exposed on the street waiting for a bus was the emergency-only option we had in place. Plan A was we'd just need a quick-smart way to get back to the train. I wanted to get to St Louis then cut back to Leland, and around to Kimball again, see what our options were over that way after I checked out the whole square block the school occupied. Fuck. I should've grabbed Mikey or RJ and come up this way a couple days ago to get this intel. My fault. Coyote *tsktsk*'d in my ear.

Central Park Avenue was still a few blocks away when we ran into the rest of our set. I wasn't sure why, because if they followed my directions, they'd be on Central Park instead of Wilson, but here we were. Jeeeezus Christ. Somedays ain't nobody follows directions, but sometimes it's all good.

"What's up, Folks?" I looked around the set, counted heads. They were short one. An important one.

"Where's RJ?" I asked.

"Whut?" said Pepper.

I looked at the Tic Tac–sized blotches across his face, marveled at their dead maple leaf color. Fall literally skittered across this luck-about-to-run-out peckerwood's face. I wondered if he could see it run away at the end of his turned-up whiteboy nose. "Jesus fuckin' Christ, man, pay attention. Where's RJ?" I repeated through my teeth under my own big wide nose.

"He ain't here."

"No shit, asshole. Where did he go?"

Hector rubbed the back of his big old neck, said, "He got busted."

"No fuckin' way."

"Yup." He rested his hand back there, his massive bicep twitching, the tattooed end of a cigarette blowing smoke from a bent-right-eared Playboy Bunny's mouth just visible, the swirls jumping along.

"Goddamnit."

"We stopped in this Iranian convenience store, grabbed a couple things. RJ even snatched a pack of Swisher Sweets from the display when old boy turned around to ring us up."

"You bought stuff?" I asked.

"Yeah," Hector said. "I got a Gatorade." He held up a sweaty yellow-green 32-ounce glass bottle with his other hand, just like in the commercials.

"Did he get caught ripping off?"

"No. We were cool, got away clean. Matter of fact, he was pulling a Honey Bun out of his jock when the man showed up out of nowhere. A regular squad car. Told us to freeze over the PA, then got out talkin' 'bout 'grab some wall, boys,' the usual bullshit. Same as back home."

"Okay. Then what?"

"They started asking us where we lived."

"The standard crap, yeah. But you guys were prepared, right?" Fuck, I thought. The El stop must not be deep enough in their neighborhood for us to be covered. And these were whiteboys, so yeah. What the fuck. Hmmm.

"For real, Midget. We were. Henry made us pick out of the phone book."

"I believe you. What's your address?"

"3742 W. Eastwood." He took a long drink from the bottle, snapped the cap down the street with his thumb and forefinger.

"Nice." I nodded at both.

"Like Clint. That's a cool street name," he said.

"True that," I agreed. "Then what?"

"I had 4632 N. St Louis Avenue," Pepper butted in.

"Of course you did, hillbilly, with your traitor state. That ain't interesting innyway. Psycho, I ain't worried about you. You're straight, I'm sure." He smirked from under his blond bangs. Henry laughed.

"Then what?" I said again. "What about RJ?"

Hector finished off the Gatorade, aaaahhhed, said, "He told 'em a address."

"And?"

"And they laughed and threw him in the backseat," he said.

"Shit. What did he tell them?"

Pepper blurted out, all proud, "I 'membered the street number. I heard him tell the cops."

"What was it?"

"4412 N. Pulaski Road."

"Wait. By Montrose? Why the fuck did he pick something all the way out there? It's on the other side of the school."

"He said you said something about Polacks, so he musta took it to heart, picked Pulaski."

"4412 North?" I double-checked.

"Yeah, man."

Dang it. I ran through spots just north of Montrose Avenue on the west side of the street. In Chicago, even numbers are on the west side of north-south streets, odds are on the east side. But that was all commercial properties. And there was only one place it could be that close to the corner.

"Shiiiiit," I said, shook my head.

"What?" Pepper and Hector chorused.

I laughed out loud. Kept laughing. Doubled over with all my hair hanging down. Caught my breath, threw my head back, and said, "RJ's about to spend the night at Belmont and Western because he memorized the address of a fuckin' Wendy's."

They looked at each other, blinked.

Then they busted out laughing, too.

We made our way toward C/P/W and the big meeting. All together now, we were a little scary given our numbers, but it was a weekday and folks in this neighborhood were at work this time of day. We ghosted through spaces that would have had three or five DP or Polack dads calling the cops on the weekend. I always thought that immigrants to the U.S. got a handbook that taught them how to say two things: "Fuck you!" and "I call the police!" Little old ladies peeked out of their hot, hot apartment sunporches, saving on the light bill with their shut windows and old-world lace curtains, dust-crusted box fans wheezing in the long hallways every one of these Chicago postwar three- and six-flats had between the front door and the living room. I knew what the insides of their apartments looked like; we had burgled more of them than I could add up, and I had Honors Math one time.

I hung back, kept the head count, watched for fellas thinking about straying off to break into cars, checked out the occasional porch for things not nailed down. Everyone was mostly keeping to the path, staying on the sidewalk, talking shit as we walked west, not idling too bad. We were still an hour and a half from meeting time.

"What you thinking about, Teddy?" Mikey said, catching up to me.

"Nothing, Folks." I was packing a new pack of smokes on the heel of my hand as I went.

"You lie." He grinned wide. "You're always thinking about something."

"Mikey, what we gonna do with our lives? Get married, have kids?"

"I don't know, Folks. Prob'ly." He rubbed his head. "You for real thinking about that shit right now?"

"Is that what you want?" I asked.

"I don't know."

"Maybe you don't know now, but do you ever wonder?" I opened my smokes, put the gold twisty in my change pocket, remembering my grandpa who liked to burn them in his ashtray, hoped I'd see him soon, then threw the rest of the plastic packaging over my shoulder.

"Thought you Injuns cried about litter and shit," Mikey said.

"You watch too much TV, brother," I said. "So do you ever wonder?" I asked again.

"No." He slapped his hands on both sides of his face a couple-three times.

"But you had an answer when I asked, said 'prob'ly,' so you do."

He laughed. "Man, fuck you. Get out of my head. That ain't cool."

I laughed back. "But you do. You think about this shit, homes, don't you?"

"Not really."

"Don't play it off like you don't think, bro. You're smart. You can see what's comin'."

"Stop fucking with me."

"I ain't fucking with you. If you didn't want to talk about it, you wouldn't have asked."

"True, I guess."

"Guess, nothing. You do want to talk about it. You want one of these?" I offered him a Marlboro Red.

"Not really. Not all that much." He took one of the smokes, patted his pockets for a light.

"Bullshit, bro. It's okay. This shit they got planned for us, work, family, death, yeah, you see it. And you know it ain't right, ain't all there is."

"Don't be getting deep on me, Midget."

"I ain't getting deep, I'm just talking about the shit I know you're thinking 'bout, too. We're getting older. Ain't got no education, even less prospects. What're we supposed to do?"

"Fine, homes. Say we got prospects after all, say you're in charge. Then what?" He packed his smoke on the back of his hand.

"You got a good mind, brother. I say you go to college." I lit my cigarette.

"Ha. For what?"

"For whatever you want. Expand that mind."

"It don't work that way, Folks." He leaned forward for me to light his square.

"But it does, if I'm in charge, like you said."

"For real? You'd send me to college?"

"I would, man."

"School ain't for me. Maybe for you, but not me." He blew a smoke ring, laughed.

"That's bullshit. That's how they want you to think. Like you got nothing to say, nothing to contribute. And that ain't right."

"You got too much faith in us, Teddy."

"All the faith I got left, I put in us, brother." I blew a ring of my own. "And I ain't going to college, neither."

"I'm getting a headache."

"But that's what you wanted, wasn't it?"

He laughed loud, and abrupt. "I guess so. You always nail it, Midget."

"That's one of my jobs, brother."

"I'm glad it's yours and not mine." He rubbed at his hair.

"Yeah, someone's gotta do the job. And you don't want it." I winked, tilted my head.

"Ain't no lie."

MIKEY

I understood what he said to me, but I don't understand why he said it to me. I'm just a regular dude off the street, but he's always talking to me about going to college and shit like that. I know I ain't dumb, but I ain't smart like he thinks I am, at least as far as school goes.

We've been bros for years, but I always think he gives me more credit than I deserve. Might be right, might be wrong, but that's how it is. He doesn't care, doesn't give a shit what our teachers think, what they tell us. He believes in us and always tells me the teachers think they're smarter than they are. I'm not sure how or why he has such confidence, but he always does, and there's no shaking that shit. We don't have much to believe in ourselves, and no one believes in us at all, except Teddy, and his commitment is a hundred percent. Fuck. It's wild to have someone like that who's our age, but for real, more of us appreciate it than will ever admit. He has no idea we do. We never tell him, but yeah, it means something to us.

TEDDY

We kept walking, all of us together now. Not gonna bullshit you, I was a little worried, kept an eye out for cops, but they weren't showing. I thought long and hard what it would be like to live in this part of town. Chicago was weird that way; every neighborhood was its own little village and every one of them was different, with its own rules, customs, and vibe. This tiny spot on the Northwest

Sice between the El and the branch at C/P/W was mostly quiet, family-like. I wasn't sure what cops in a neighborhood like this did all day, probably hung out in donut shops and told stale-ass jokes to each other. I know I would if I was a cop. I wondered if there was a Huck Finn out this way; hands down they were the best donut joint in the city. They made their shit in the window for everyone to see and they for real had the best grease going. There was one under the Howard Street El the old man would go to on special occasions, you know, like when he got too drunk and did some stupid shit he had to make up for, and I knew there'd be another one on Archer Avenue from when I'd live out on the South Side in a decade or so.

As soon as we crossed Drake we got made. There were lookouts on every corner, in a ton of wide-open apartment windows. This was a big set, even bigger than I thought, and they had this place on lock. I took a pile of mental notes. There were gonna be some changes back home. We'd need to collect some dues, or sell more weed, rent cribs on our corners, turn out some landlords. This shit was tight. This was how you did it.

A couple of their Peewees looked us up and down, took off on their bikes. Making for their warlord, I figured. I'd check in with my counterpart later, make sure their intel was up to speed, head count, descriptions, whatnot. They moved with a purpose. Knew we weren't opposition, but still needed to let their folks know we were here. I appreciated their respect for their responsibilities, and us.

No shit, maybe thirty or forty seconds later a couple of Juniors came out the front door of a six-flat on the south side of Wilson. Two dark-haired dudes, at least one a whiteboy, both with medium-length feathered hair wearing dago Ts, light blue baggies, and black suede roller bottoms pulled up to us, flashing the crossed fingers of American Sign Language Rs and saying, "Royal Love, what's up, Folks?"

"R-Love. T/R, F/C. King Killer, Queen Thriller. Ain't no pity in Simon City," I replied, smiled.

The rest of the fellas responded, "Royals! Farwell and Clark. Touhy and Ridge! What's up, Folks?"

"Ain't nothing but a thing. You see it, Folks," the mass of white-boys called back.

"Alright, Folks." We met on the sidewalk, shook hands Royal-style: soul, four fingers, forefinger gun twisted to pitchforks, snapped fingers, thumb, forefinger and pinky matched to make a crown thrown upside down.

"Royal." Eyes met.

"Royal." Stares in return.

"Alright, Folks. Welcome to Central Park and Wilson."

"Cool, cool, Folks. Appreciate it."

"Ain't nothing but a thang, Folks," the shorter one said. I figured him for the warlord. I was right. He might've been Native, was probably Italian. Whatever.

"Y'all are kinda early, Midget." He knew my name, that sort of thing being the business of warlords and other officers.

"Cain't fuck around when it comes to this, Little Man," I said, knew his right back. "It's an important meeting. No CPT here. No Indian Time, no Colored People Time, know what I'm saying?" I liked watching whiteboys wrap their head around the new shit they needed to know about the alliances they made with Native and Black and brown folks.

"True, true," he said. "I appreciate the respect."

"I thought you might," I said. "Much respect, Folks." Wasn't no point in fucking around. Like I said, this was a big set, and if we ever needed some assistance, there wasn't no harm in establishing good relations. They had a pile of whiteboys who were ready to follow orders. Our hood was getting a little wild; lots of Kings 🖐 and Vice Lords 🜨 moving in. Man. They were busing those dudes in from the West Side at school. We might need these brothers pretty soon. We were a Nation, yeah, but still, our set came first. And if these mugs could put a body on some of these Coronas and Vickie Lous, well alright, Folks. I was willing to be a diplomat every now and again, know what I'm saying?

They looked at our set, most of the whiteboys on one side, and the rest of us on the other. I watched them calculate, check out the muscle, assess what we had going on. No shit, we were formidable. I wouldn't fuck with us.

I broke the awkward.

"So what's up, Folks? What do we do until the meeting?"

"I ain't know, Folks," the little warlord said. "We could chill in the crib for a minute. Want to come up?"

"Yeah. That'll work, Folks. What do you think, fellas?" I asked.

Lots of "alrights" and "cool, Folks" floated up.

"There it is," I said.

"Alright, then," Little Man said. "Let's get it." He slid to the front door.

"Let's hit it," I said.

"Cool, cool, Folks," he said.

We followed him through the building's front door and up through the first-floor door on the right-hand side. It led to a typical giant NW Side Chicago apartment, a couple bedrooms, big living room up front, kitchen, dining room, and bed and bathroom in the back. We waltzed down the little hallway to the left with some old-world black-and-white pictures then into the living room with its sunporch, windows wide open to the street.

"Hey now, Folks. This is cool," I said.

"It's alright," Little Man said, his assistant still not saying a word.

"Nah. For real. This shit is tight," I said, running my fingers through my hair.

"It's cool, Folks," he said.

"Alright, Folks," I said. "Alright."

"Wanna get high and watch cartoons?" he said.

"For real? What's even on right now?" I said. "Probably just soap operas, yeah?"

"Nah, homes. We got a VCR with a bunch of Tom and Jerry cartoons we taped."

I had heard of those machines but never seen one. "Fuck yeah, homes. Let's do it," I said.

"Alright, Folks," he said, and threw a huge bag of weed on the coffee table in the living room.

Little Man

My ancestors want me to spit some Irish at this Indian-looking motherfucker, but I can't string two sentences together; my ma never taught me and my da says the language is useless here. I think it would at least be good for us to talk shit when the pigs are around, but no one ever bothers. I probably could press my uncle, but we never have the time for it anyway. They're all from the Old Country, from the West, and have the language, but it's fading from them fast. I hear the Provos are using it to talk to each other in the Maze up North. Crazy harsh reason to keep the tongue alive, but whatever it takes, I suppose. I wish they'd teach it to me, but I'll have to pick up bits and pieces where I can. It makes me mad this Indian cat probably still has his, but I can't resent him— these American fucks have stolen so much from them they're lucky to have whatever they have left.

Anyway, it's a big day trying to host all these motherfuckers. Vinnie and I have our hands full with these guys. Johnny says it was important to do it right, but we don't know any of these broth-

ers. Some of them look pretty rugged. Their one warlord is something else. I heard he came over from another branch, some senior
dudes who went defunct. His little ass marches around barking
orders and keeping fellas in line. I need to keep notes; I have no
idea how he keeps it all together, but he does.

Mikey

Holy shit. I'm high as fuck. I'm trying to think about what I'm
gonna say to Juanita tonight, tryna finesse my business but I can't
concentrate. Everybody is watching cartoons all loud and shit,
just chillin' so that was cool, but what a weird house. All the front
windows are wide open, full of Peewees on patrol. The living room
is huge. No overhead light or rugs on the floor, just a couple shitty
lamps on cheap side tables and two ratty couches that slide on
hardwood floors every time someone sits down or gets up, but
there are beautiful built-in shelves and an ornate mantel around a
dead fireplace, every space filled with framed black-and-white Old
Country people. The walls have framed funeral cards and more old
dead white folks. I couldn't imagine living in a shrine like this, a
mausoleum full of faces that stare at you like you'd forgotten their
names and are pissed about it, but that's the whole mood in this
room and the rest of the house, the vibe like yeah, once upon a
time we were strong, and we were family. Remember that shit.

Teddy

We got high, some of the boys more than others. I gave out the
stares when they were hitting it too hard, but what can you do?
I hit the bowl a couple times myself, being polite but not really

wanting to get any higher. You *cannot* fuck around during times like these. I knew it was gonna be a bit before the meeting, so I was hoping it would wear off. Still, when that one came on where Tom is a cowboy rolling his own square trying to impress the girl cat and smokes his own face off, we all just fell out laughing. Man, I love that episode.

"Hey, bro, y'all got anything to drink around here? Pop or juice or some?" I asked.

"Yeah," Little Man said. "There's a bunch of shit in the fridge. Help yourself."

"Alright. Thanks."

Walking the hallway toward the kitchen, I looked at framed photos of ancient Irish widows and shit, wondered who all the fuck lived here. Probably had an old grandma stashed in the back room. Some of these big-ass apartments had servants' quarters from back in the day. A bedroom and little bathroom off the kitchen behind the pantry. That was where the aging relatives in these white ethnic families ended up.

Yup. This was one of those. As soon as I saw the dead gaslight fixtures capped off on the wall by the back door I knew. Coming into the kitchen proper, there was a small painted-over delivery door next to the window by the pantry where the butler or the maid could get the stuff for breakfast. I wondered what it would be like to have milk and eggs and butter brought to your house every day by some dude dressed in all white, with a little captain hat and a corny old-school farm truck. Probably pretty cool, actually.

And now I was worried about the grandma or uncle or whatever they had going on here. I was sure I'd find someone in the back bedroom. Fuck. What if they had some horrible illness and shit? But as I thought about someone dying back here, it occurred to me that they'd have some pills to ease their journey into the next world. Codeine at least. Maybe even morphine. Alright. Let's check it out.

I crept down the little hallway toward the open bathroom door that let in tons of natural light. I could see a claw-foot tub with a teal-and-white-striped towel hanging over the edge and a floor made of those tiny six-sided tiles that always did the optical illusion thing when you stared too long while you were sitting on the can. The bedroom door on the right was half-open, and I could hear a box fan thundering along inside. I leaned my head to the left trying to peek in before I got seen by whoever was in the room. I didn't make a sound; the bottoms of my high-tops were worn paper-thin.

Holy shit. There was a thousand-year-old human lumped under a pile of blankets on a pair of mattresses with no headboard. I couldn't tell if it was a man or a woman, even when they spoke. And speak they did as soon as I got halfway through the door for a closer look.

"Kay hay toosa! Imick lee at!" they yelled over the theme song to *All My Children.*

What the fuck. I had a buddy whose uncle was from the Old Country, this language when he got super shit-faced. It was Irish, for sure. Confirmed Little Man wasn't Native or Italian. He was Black Irish.

"Sorry! Sorry," I said. I didn't know to say grandma or uncle, so I left it plain. "I'm a friend of . . . Brendan's," I guessed. "I was just looking for the bathroom."

"It's right there, eejit! What are ya, feckin' blind?!" they yelled.

"Right on, mamó!" I hollered back.

A whole string of angry Irish popped out, so I knew I got the gender wrong. "You want me to close the door? Okay, then," I said.

"No! Don't close the—"

Too late.

I turned to the bathroom and peeped the medicine cabinet.

Whoa. A filmy prescription of Numorphan *and* a couple bottles of cough syrup with codeine.

Score.

As soon as this weed wore off, yeah. I'm hittin' this shit. I stuffed my pockets.

Understand, when it comes to gangbanging, opiates and pot inhabit entirely different worlds. Especially if you get into a humbug. Then, being pumped full of syrup is like a superpower. Sure, you pay for it later if you get whomped on, but with weed, you can get rocked. Fuck that.

I slunk back out to the kitchen, poked my head in the fridge. Lots of margarine tubs with what I imagined were weird leftovers, probably potatoes, corned beef, and cabbage, shit like that. There were ketchup and Chinese mustard packets in the butter drawer on the door, a couple of eggs, and some moldy cheese in the deli compartment. There was a quarter jug of orange juice with pulp, ew, so no go there, an unopened quart of RC from some pizza delivery no doubt, and a half-empty two liter of Pepsi. I grabbed the RC, the glass bottle icy on my hand, sticking to my skin. I looked in the cupboards for something to pour it into, but the sink full of dishes and margarine bowls told me that the whole of their china service was out of commission at the moment. I carried the bottle out of the kitchen and down the hallway, cracking it open as I went. I paused next to what must've been a photo of the old man in the back room in his prime, smiling next to a dock, probably on his way to America, took a big drink and burped. I put the cap back on and bounced into the living room.

"Anybody want some of this pop?" I sat back down on the couch.

"Fuck yeah, homes," Mikey said, eyes just red.

"Here you go, bro." I handed him the bottle. "Pass it around."

"Thomas!" the TV screamed.

I loved the aunties on this show. One of them went after our boy with her broom.

"Alright, Little Man," I said, settling on the couch. "Tell me some things about this branch."

Most of these guys still lived at home. That tracked. Shit, I had an Irish buddy whose thirty-six-year-old brother was a Chicago cop and lived at home. His parents were from the Old Country, his mom made him sandwiches on command and did his laundry. Why would he ever move out? Most of their parents knew what was up, and the money my pal made from slinging dope helped pay the rent and sent a little back home. Old Country rules and immigrant mistrust of the cops were the rule of the day. Even the cats who were old-school Chicago had parents who maintained that code. The whole neighborhood was on lock; dads ran gambling joints and the moms helped with the numbers. It was a society unto itself. I could appreciate that.

"Respect, bro. I dig your setup."

"Much love, Folks," Little Man said.

"We ain't got it like this," I said.

"Nothin' but a thing, Folks. To each his own. I'm sure you all got whatever works for you," he said.

"Yeah," I said, "but it could be better."

"It could always be better, homes, but I know you know that."

"For real, Folks. Just trying to make it all work." I was suddenly reflective and thoughtful. What the fuck. I wished this weed would wear off so I could drop one of these Numorphans or hit that syrup.

"It's a new day out there, Folks," he said. "With this fresh Nation and shit, things are changing. It ain't like it used to be, just fuckin' with the rednecks and whatnot. Beating up Kings and G/Ls."

"Yeah, for real Folks. It's about to get really real."

"That's what this meeting'll be about, homes. We're fixin' to see a whole new world."

"Yeah?" I said, reaching in my pocket for my smokes.

"You ready?" he asked.

"Don't matter if I am or not, if we are or not, yeah?"

"Yeah," he laughed. "Ready or not, here it comes."

"Shiiiiit," I said.

"Shiiiiit," he laughed.

I flipped open my box and shook a Red his way. He took it, pulled out a baby blue Bic.

"Simon City Royals Nation's gonna be alright," he said, lighting his smoke. "Maybe even big, you know what I'm sayin'?"

"Maybe, Folks. Maybe," I said, taking the lighter when he offered it. The smoke curled up, and I thought some of this might reach Arab in the afterlife, wherever he was. I hoped he would see this.

We were about to become bigger than we ever dreamed. Years later, we'd be on CNN, and they'd be talking about branches of our thing down in Mississippi for fuck's sake. You can say what you want about the goofy whiteboy greasers who started it all, but Simon City and our founders like Arab (that's a long A at the front) saw from the jump the whole white alliance thing was bunk, that the future was mixed, that their future, *our* future depended on cross-racial bonds, just like America if *it* wants to have a future, and here we'd be, three or four decades later, a thoroughly mixed and badass set calling the shots in multiple states, multiple prisons; our thing surviving when plenty of other sets had died out. Yeah, I could see it then, and though maybe I couldn't articulate it, I for real knew its value, saw it in action every damn day. Simon City, motherfucker. Ain't no pity.

I had the newspaper clipping from when Arab got killed by Insane Deuces like five years previously, in 1974, but don't remember which paper it was from. The *Tribune* was conservative and would have run it to complain about crime and shit; the *Daily*

News was the paper I liked and seemed to be about regular folks like the *Sun-Times,* which picked up most of its readers when the *Daily News* folded. Whoever it was, they got his name wrong, the fucking assholes. It was Rashad. Anyway, it looked like this, probably from the *Chicago Daily News:*

2 SEIZED IN GANG-TIE SLAYINGS

By Phillip Wattley

ARRESTS HAVE been made in the separate slayings of Vernon [Boom Boom] Baker, indicted in 1970 for the murder of two policemen, and Rasher Zayed, leader of a North Side gang, police said yesterday. Police suspect both deaths were gang-related slayings.

Doran Daniels, 18, of 6907 S. Crandon Ave., was charged with murder in the fatal shooting of Baker, 18.

Baker was one of four persons indicted in the slaying of two policemen in the Cabrini-Green housing project in 1970.

He was shot once between the eyes as he walked with his sister and brother near his home at 7030 S. Clyde Ave., Thursday.

Zayed, 25, of 3469 N. Clark St., reputed leader of the Simon City Royals, was shot Wednesday, allegedly in a territorial dispute with the Deuces gang, police said.

Charged with his murder were Edward Bartnicki, 17, of 2955 N. Damen Ave., and Gary Chavarria, 17, of 2062 N. Damen Ave., who allegedly deserted the Marine Corps last February. A 16-year-old also was charged with murder in a delinquency petition.

Another 16-year-old has been named in a delinquency petition, for the June 15 slaying of Heriberto
Hernandez, 26.

Probably more to some of us than others but still to everyone,
I think, Arab meant something, stood for something. Through
all kinds of bullshit, bunches of scabby racist crap and hardcore
family beliefs, Arab knew there was something better, and all we
needed to do was understand we had more in common than different; those *differences* were put in place to keep us apart, to keep
us distracted and from getting what we deserved, too.

He was one of those people, and we know what happens to
them . . .

Rashad Zayed was murdered by a couple of seventeen-year-old
marine deserter Deuces a few days after his twenty-fifth birthday
and a few years before most of us joined, so he was full legend by
then. If it wasn't scumbag Deuces, it would've been Unknowns,
or Kings, or cops, no matter. His days were numbered. Our society can't handle truth tellers, not the ones who can bring folks
together, anyway.

Once you're gone, it's up to those left behind to tell your story.
Keep your fingers crossed and hope they get it right, or get it
glorious, depending on what you're into. All you can do is write
as much of your own story that'll stick before everyone else gets a
chance at it.

If they even remember you.

All a that ran though my head, but of course I just said, "You
want some of that pop, homes?"

"Alright," Little Man said.

"Mikey, send the RC back over this way," I said.

He took it from Pepper, mid-chug, the greedy white fucker.

"Here you go, Folks," Mikey said, handing me the bottle. I gave it to Little Man.

"Alright, bro," he said, tipping it back.

I watched him drink, thought about everyone who had hit that bottle.

"You good, Folks?" he asked, finishing it off, setting the empty on the table.

"All good, Folks," I said, looking over at an unwound antique mantel clock. "Should we get moving? What's the time?"

"You worried?" He laughed.

"Nah, bro," I said. "Just keeping an eye on things."

"Right on, Midget," he said. "No worries. Let's pull up."

"Alright, Folks," I raised my voice a little. "Let's head out."

Little Man snapped off the cartoons with the clicker.

"Let's go, Folks," he said to his crew.

Everyone gathered up their smokes, lighters, beers. We drifted to the door.

"Okay, Uncle John!" he yelled. "We're leaving!"

A string of muffled Irish wafted our way.

I shook my head, turned my back to the set, pulled out one of the codeine bottles, took a double drink. "Right on, boys. Let's go."

"What was that they said?" Mikey asked Little Man.

"Nothing homes. Old Country stuff. It don't matter."

"Alright," Mikey said. "Alright."

Down the musty stairs and out the front door. Now we were about thirty dirty gangbangers. This kind of mob action would get us all busted toot suite in our neighborhood, but these guys didn't seem worried in the least.

"Hey, Little Man. We good boppin' down the street like this?" I asked.

"Yeah. All good, Folks. No worries."

"Alright, then," I said.

"Follow me," he said. "Need to stop by the garage. We're hooking you up."

We went down a walkway on the side of the building toward the back. It opened up into a brick shithouse of a garage, at least a four-car. It was huge.

"Come on, homes," he said.

I was a little apprehensive, but these cats were cool so far.

"Let's go, boys," I said, sensing the same worry in my set.

We walked in through an off-white-milk-enamel-painted door.

"Holy shit," I said.

This garage was like the world's best clubhouse. Two refrigerators, a '71 'Cuda, tons of tools, stacks of *Playboys,* what the fuck. This was crazy. Then Little Man pointed.

"Grab a bat, fellas. We're just off to play some softball."

No shit. There was a rack with like forty baseball bats up against a side wall.

"Damn, boys. Lookit that. Grab a bat."

"For real, homes?" Hector asked.

"For real," I said. "Yeah, Little Man?"

"Yeah," he said. "Have at it, bro." He tossed a grubby sixteen-inch Clincher back and forth.

"Damn. Get it, Folks," I said.

Everyone grabbed a bat.

This was the goods.

We headed out.

Little Man

We'll see what happens. Johnny wants this all to come off right, like we look like the main set, the ones calling the shots, but these way-far North Side motherfuckers kinda strut around like they own the place. I ain't never seen folks so cocky and these cats don't seem to give a fuck about nothing. I wonder what their neighborhood is like. I know they humbug with Kings a lot, and that Deuces and shit try to do drive-bys on them. Maybe that's why they keep it so cool, don't seem like anything bothers them. It's a wild way to be. I check them for nervous tics, but they're all chill. We got cops on our side and nothing to worry about, but for real these motherfuckers walk around like they own our neighborhood, too. Damn, man.

TEDDY

Making our way over to Roosevelt schoolyard was surreal. Thirty armed dudes, all from the same club? That was like the size of an army platoon, but we were soldiers for our own thing. That had meaning, whether we realized it or not. There'd never be another day like this one, even if we didn't appreciate it then. We talked *toza* shit on the way, said things that should've been immortalized. We laughed and joked the whole time, never having felt this invincible ever before, it was amazing. We swung our bats around at each other, at fences, garbage cans.

A squad car drifted by. The uniform gave us a nod. This shit was crazy.

"Little Man, do y'all pay off the cops or what?"

"We don't have to," he said. "Plenty of them are in the set or at least used to be."

Holy fuck. I couldn't even imagine. Cops were the worst opposition we had.

"For real, homes?" I asked.

"Yeah. For real," he said.

Damn, I thought.

Damn. Damn. Damn. That's a hell of a thing. We needed to do the same. Cops on the payroll or in the set was the way to go. I'd buy great coke off cops one day, but this was a-whole-nother level.

"Right on," I said.

Little Man's assistant was a couple steps behind us, walking backward, keeping an eye on it all.

"How's it going back there?" I asked.

"Good, good, Folks," he said.

"Right on," I said.

"Alright," his boss threw in.

"So, where you from Little Man?" I asked, still wondering if maybe this cat was at least part Native, just lived with some Irish family. His accent was from here, though.

"What do you mean, homes? You were at my crib."

Nope. Never mind. Not Native for sure, 'cause that question has definite answers.

"Ah, just wondering if you grew up around here or whatever," I said, covering.

"Yeah. My parents came over on the boat, you know?" he said.

Black Irish, then, for sure. Oh well. All good.

"That's cool, bro," I said. "You got your language still?"

"Nah, man. Too much work, you know? I got a few words, but whatever."

"I hear you, bro," I said.

"Yeah? Why? What's your language? You're like an Injun or something, right? Thought you guys were all gone."

"Nah, bro. We're still here," I said. "Lots of us, actually. Prolly more than y'all know, but that's alright."

"Yeah?"

"Yeah," I said, trying to end that conversation.

"You ain't mad, are you, bro?" he kept it up.

"About what?" I up-nodded at him.

'About all this . . . ?" He held his hands out wide.

"All what? All this shit? These motherfuckers running around like they found the joint? Nah, man. It is what it is. What can you do?"

"You can do what we're fixin' to do right now. Take back some of it anyway," he said.

Dude was in my head a little bit. I didn't like it.

"Yeah, homes. Take some back," I agreed.

"Last of the Mohicans, Folks, right?" he offered.

"Something like that." I took a big look at the sky, finished my smoke, flicked it in the street, kinda wished we had brought the boom box, 'cause right now I woulda jacked the volume.

Folks might've felt invincible, and I wanted to feel that, too. Acted like it right along with them, but I knew maybe a little bit better that it ain't so good to get that cocky, that we gotta be respectful, too, think about everyone who got us here, kept us here, needed us to keep going. Coyote modeled that for Native folks, showed us what not to do, sure, but he made us think about the why not, and that was the lesson that was supposed to stick, whether any of us knew it or not. How when you're doing for just yourself you're doing it wrong, and what those consequences could be. He showed me how to sit and just be, and though it sounds corny, he said in order to achieve, you have to conceive and then believe. And yeah, for real, that works for everyday stuff you want to get done, all the time yo, but in there is a lesson at the conceive it part. If you do it right, if you . . . *enter* it, really float in it, the ways to get there seep in on the sides of the vision, and you can *see* the future. It's a little scary at first, but man, it's the real deal. Doing that, being open to those bleeds that swirl in? That's how you see what's coming. Maybe you make adjustments, do things that bring those moments in, and you don't realize it, but they happen. Your job is to remember them, put them all together, and use them as your guide. All of a sudden you *know* what's going to happen. He taught me that. I always paid attention to the things he said, but that time I concentrated real hard.

I had thought a lot about what might happen today, but shit's on me—I didn't think of a path beyond keeping folks safe, getting the thing done. And right now was too late to start. I rolled with the giddiness that brought, not knowing the short future, rode everyone else's vibe, wondered what Coyote would do and knew he'd say, *Fuck it. Let's go, boys.*

We rolled into Roosevelt. Holy shit.

The schoolyard was huge, a massive blacktop with basketball hoops here and there, but at least a quarter of a square city block, multiple redbrick school buildings with hundreds of those old-style super tall windows looming in the background, a light breeze and a beautiful sun smiling down on everything and everyone. And it was filled with Royals from every branch, along with some Popes, Disciples, and the stray Folks they'd brought along to beef up their size. Not gonna lie. It was something else.

You have to understand—this was some Hollywood-level shit for us. Yeah, I'd seen *The Warriors* ten times at least by then in a couplethree different theaters and I know what this sounds like, but I also knew what I was looking at. Unprecedented. We're talking three or four hundred members of the new Nation including at least two hundred and fifty Royals; this was a massive gathering of our Folks. All the sets were here. Us from Farwell and Clark / Touhy and Ridge, along with representatives from Christiana and Wellington, Central Park and Wilson, Kenmore and Leland, Southport and Fullerton, Albany and School, Paulina and Cornelia, Bell schoolyard, and maybe Koz Park and a couple Eddy Street

Seniors. Sure, I know now we have branches and hella members across the country, but in 1979, well damn, this was huge. And this was pre-internet, pre-cellphone, pre-everything; we were some old-school Stone Age motherfuckers getting it together, talking about our thing, our non-racist we're-all-brothers vibe, street interpretation of Cosa Nostra. That's impressive, I don't care who you are.

A few squad cars rolled by now and again; we made like we were setting up a softball game to keep things looking legit. Old people neighbors sat on their stoops and porches, looked out their windows at us, but it was low-key. I watched them when some of the Black Gangster Disciples rolled in, clocked the tension and hands that waved around in conversation, but no one went back in to call the cops or anything. A couple of the C/P/W boys made their way down the row of houses and apartments, jabbered in Irish or Polish or DP or hillbilly, whatever they needed to calm these folks down. We were in good shape.

Johnny, then CoCo, then a couple of section presidents made speeches, handed out how it was gonna be, tried to get the boys fired up a little. I shifted on my feet, wanting so much to hear some inspiration, some reason to get excited about soldiering, keeping up our part of the Nation, but it started to feel a whole lot like what RJ was talking about earlier; these big shots were gonna mouth around about how it was gonna be all the while thinking about what they were gonna make off the deals.

Yawn.

And I wasn't the only one. I could tell the boys were that worst thing you could get—disappointed. We were old-school gangbangers. Liked to humbug, sling a little dope, party, talk shit. This was turning into a business meeting.

Since business meeting seemed to be the vibe, I decided to conduct one myself. I up-nodded to a couple of bros I knew from the Northwest branches, Royals who had come down to parties in our neighborhood. I recognized one guy and his buddy from the time we were getting it on at this crib by Paschen Park, and a couple of undercover crackers got drunk enough to start yelling "GL! Gaylords! Royal killer!" thinking there were only a couple of white ones there. Yeah. These two were like fuck all that and six or eight of us from different races and branches beat the white power right out of those GLs.

These guys had the hookup on some ARs that had been ganked from a National Guard armory up in their hood. We shook hands, dropped the crown, laughed about those Gaylords at the party, and then I did the whole "Hey, Folks, can you look out for us with some of that government equipment," and they were like, "Oh yeah, for sure, Folks, we need to party again soon anyway," and we made a deal 'cause that's what you do. I said my alright laters / stay up, Folks, and faded back to my set, listened to all the preaching up front with my mind on getting that firepower in our hands, fuzzing out on that cheerleading shit and making plans for the pickup.

The speechifying went on for a while. We listened to details that seemed to me to benefit the dudes who thought they were in charge; we'd have all kind of new reporting structures and dues and payments—sounded like an Amway pyramid scam to me. When bureaucrats fuck around with folks who get things done it all turns to shit. I failed to see how any of this would benefit our set. We just shared mostly everything and took care of each other. I started to peace out just like I'd do in meetings for the rest of my life, learning early on that "meetings" were just an excuse for people in love with the sound of their own voice to inflict it on people who'd rather be doing anything else.

In between the blah-blah it got so quiet you could hear the occasional train screech into the station. During one of the downtimes Mikey got bored and decided to do some smoke rings. There was no breeze here between the arms of the building, so he did that thing where you take a huge drag, O your mouth, then tap-tap-tap your finger on your cheek, blow out about forty little smoke rings. They hung in the air, clashed into each other like a bowl of SpaghettiOs. Some of the boys laughed, but in that restless, nervous way you do when you're bored. Fuck. Yeah. We were gangbangers, not the fuckin' sales team. The fellas were losing interest fast, and we started to drift toward the back of things along the fence at Leland, away from the main crowd up by the big talkers in front of the main building.

I kept thinking about how we had to truck all the way up here through a bunch of enemy territory, so this was kind of bullshit. I wasn't totally resentful, but still, I was responsible for all these guys, so yeah, there was that. We'd have to talk about the value of ever doing some shit like this again. Coyote whispered with a wink from somewhere to remind me about community, sure, but to be looking out for my own first. Sure enough, it all of a sudden felt like we should peace out early, unnoticed. Beat the rush.

Pop.

Pop-pop-pop.

What the fuck? Those were shots. Careful what you wish for, I guessed. Shit. I looked around and there was a tank on Leland, a big Tootsie Pop orange '72 Gran Torino with a greasy blond long-haired whiteboy who looked like a fat-faced jack of diamonds from a waterlogged pack of Hoyle's hanging out the side window squeezing off shots with a shitty little pistol. He was wearing a Palmer Street party sweater, too; I could see the knit gray sleeves with black cuffs at the wrist.

Of course nobody got hit, so everyone yelled "Gaylord Killer" and started rushing the beater, ball bats in hand. Finally! Something to do. He only had a couple shots left and obviously couldn't shoot for shit, so no one was worried. Ten or twelve Royals jumped the little four-foot fence and ran after the car. I didn't think the big faces up front even knew what was happening—the sounds of the shots from the cheap piece were lost in all their talking. I hung back and kept an eye on things.

And was glad I did because fuck! here came the cops, six or eight unmarked squads and shit, paddy wagons galore. They used a kind of simple pincer movement, coming up Leland from the east and St Louis from the south, trying to surround us. I saw some Area 6 Gang Intelligence I knew. Fucking cop snitches. A lot of them A6 GIs were Vietnam vets who used to be Taylor Street Jousters and Gaylords, those white power fucks with patchy mustaches. I felt sorry for their neglected girlfriends as the schoolyard erupted in chaos, Folks tearing ass in fifty different directions, warlords and presidents from up front jumping into action, trying to direct traffic north and west, doing a pretty good job, just like in the movie.

And just like in the movie, I knew this shit was coming, so I sent my boys the other way, against the grain. We had an emergency plan worked out the day I told them about this meeting, a plan for what to do if the cops showed up. Once we cleared the schoolyard, we'd break into twos and threes, meet at Montrose and Kedzie instead of Kimball, in case they needed to take alleys and whatnot to get to Montrose. Once we got there, we'd make our way east down the avenue, keeping close to the buildings until a bus came. Then we could get to the Ravenswood stop and head to Belmont, transferring to an Englewood–Jackson Park to get us back home; Morse was an all-stops, so any train would do. The F/C and T/R boys moved out south, toward Wilson, then Montrose, and beyond. I did a quick head count; found we were missing one.

And I looked and of course there was Lil Psycho down the street, emptying his whole clip into that Gran Torino, yelling at the top of his Lugan lungs, God love him.

LiL PSYCHO

I was just fucking around, smoking a cigarette back by the chain-link fence that went around the whole schoolyard, talking to Lil Capone about what a scene this whole thing was when I saw the beater cruising up slow down the street. I had a weird feeling about it, looked at him, and said get ready homes, some shit's about to go down. He was like, for real? Yeah, I said. Check it out.

Man, I have no idea how I got hooked up with these dudes in the first place, but hell yeah, it's a good time. I knew Teddy from somewhere else first, probably a concert. We dig tunes together and shit, talk about books and whatnot, but I had no idea he was into this gangbanging shit so deep until it was too late. I go to school at Loyola. My old man pays for it; him and my ma have been divorced for a while, but he has dough, is a professor. He cares about education and so do the Jesuits, so it's private high school for me.

I don't feel like a tourist, but for real, this is the craziest anthropology class you can ever take. The theory here would be what the priests call cultural relativism, I guess, but in this context it's wild. I can, and do, tell myself I can walk away whenever I want, but really, I can't. When you commit like I did, you're in, and that's it. As long as I pull my weight, these brothers don't question shit. And that, I suppose, is what it was about. Take care of your business, and them, and they'll take care of you. Yeah, I knew I'd survive it and look back on it someday, but in the moment I'm ready to die just like they are. That'll never leave you.

I pull my pistol and start busting caps at these rednecks. Fuck, I figure. They're packing, so it's my right to pop off some shots. And yeah, nail it. This ugly doughy fucker is for real waving a piece around and squeezing the trigger. I pull until I'm out of shots. Not sure if I hit anything or not, but damn. What a rush.

TEDDY

"Psycho!" I used my big voice, the one I'd need later in boot camp. "Come on!" The cops were closing up their lil pincer move, starting to squeeze us together.

"Alright, bro," he yelled back, trying to figure out where to put his suddenly smoking-hot pistol.

I could see him struggling. "Stick it in your back pocket and let's go!" I hollered.

"I'm coming, bro!" he laughed, running and jamming the piece in the back of his pants.

I shook my head, laughing, windmilled my left arm at him. "Go, go, go!"

He caught up and we jogged over to the rest of the boys.

The last thing I heard was Little Man yelling "Vinnie!" so yeah, I guess that was his assistant's name.

All the boys moved quick across the blacktop east and south toward Kimball and Wilson against the swirling mass; I walked backward, keeping an eye on the madness over on St Louis. I saw folks getting whaled on by the cops, winced, yelled over my shoulder, "They're rounding mugs up; got Folks against hoods and whatnot, shaking everyone down!" These boys might've had the neighborhood cops on lock, but the GIs overrode their authority here. This was serious shit.

"Damn," Folks mumbled, grumbled, with headshakes; everyone kept moving, though.

"All good, Folks. Keep going," I said, as a big-mustached GI slammed Vinnie's face into the hood of a narc car. *Damn, homes,* I said to myself. *You look like an angry version of the Village People guy, and I ain't judging, but that was uncalled for.* Little Man caught my eye across the distance. I gave him an up-nod and shook my head, turned around, hustled up. The commotion stopped for a second, the way it does in those cycles of chaos, and the only sound I heard was a train coming too fast into the station a few blocks away.

The temptation to head back to the El stop at Kimball was strong, but I shook it off and stuck to the plan. It felt like they knew what we were up to, and if so, there'd be cops at the station for sure. We needed to keep going the other way.

"We good, boys?" I asked as we cleared the last bit of chain-link, stood out on the corner of Kimball and Wilson, across the street from Roosevelt. The head count told me yes, but still.

"Yeah, Folks. We're good," Henry said.

"Alright, then. What's the plan?" I asked.

"Looks like we're about that emergency plan. Montrose and Kedzie, Folks. Just like we talked about. We'll see you there," Walter said.

"Yup. Montrose and Kedzie," Pepper gulped.

"Damn straight, Folks," I said. "Twos and threes and make your way."

I watched the whiteboys clump up, stick together and head out.

Mikey popped up. "There's something to those theories of yours, Teddy." He grinned, watching the whiteboys walk away, tapping his hickory stick on the ground. I couldn't believe he still had it.

"I know, homes."

He laughed, rubbed at his hair. "Let's go, den, Folks," he said.

"Sko'," I laughed. "And get rid of those bats."

MIKEY

If those whiteboys get made and mopped out here, or busted, that'll fuck up our set for a minute. I keep an eye on them and ask them to split up, maybe one of them come with us, but they're gonna make their own way, they say. Fingers crossed or whatever, bro.

I tell Teddy them whiteboys stick together for sure. It's funny how they'll fight between themselves every chance they get but will be all united and shit around any Black or brown brothers. They're hard to figure out. I asked Teddy about it a few times, but he didn't trust whiteboys under any circumstances, so that wasn't helpful. He tells me to just stay away from them as much as I can. For real, though, we have to figure out the whiteboy thing while they're still around in any kind of numbers. Maybe the best we can hope for is that they'll slink off to the suburbs or out here to the Northwest Side. He's kinda right, I guess. They have their own ways and priorities that don't match up with ours too much. Seems like so many white folks have moved away it's only a matter of time before these ones do, too. Still, as long as they're here, we can't ignore them. Like white people everywhere, they always take up so much space.

TEDDY

Henry took off with Walter and Miguel. Not wise, I thought, to have your top three moving together as a crew, but hey, who am I to judge what other sets did? Besides, those cats had been together since they were little, so yeah, do what you have to do in strange territory. They went south on Kimball but took a right through some gangway and into the alley on the west side of the street. A little off plan, but whatever.

Two whiteboy bundles of Hector and his brother Lil Bugs moved east on Wilson with Pepper while Mikey2 and 3 followed close behind. Lil Psycho and Demon took Lil Capone south down Kimball; the rest of the set peeled off in twos and threes over to the next block, splitting between Sunnyside and its alley, and we all strolled along like we were enjoying our summer vacation or something. Me and Mikey took the first alley east on Wilson, the one that ran down Kimball. It was pretty wide open, and as an alley to a major thoroughfare, I knew we could take it as far as we wanted, with plenty of turnoffs and gangways if we needed them. Plus, it looked like most of these garage doors over here were still bare, freshly painted over. I pulled out a royal blue magnum and got ready, couldn't resist that sparkly new canvas even though we needed to get moving. It's not every day you get to throw up your set in virgin territory. I know that's some colonial bullshit, but sometimes it's like that. Vivaldi's *Le quattro stagioni* ("L'Inverno"! The only concerto Lucifer would listen to in full! Blame it on that prick Dante . . .) burst into my head, so that was always a good sign. I put up some of my best work, super detailed with bent-eared, top-hatted bunnies and X-eyed suicide Kings and dead Klansmen with lots of T/R crosses so their little scouts on bikes would know it was us when they reconned after all this shit was over. Mikey took out his black Sanford, gave it a sniff and shaded in all my 3D work, added some F/C crosses of his own. I was excited about what might be coming our way and nervous for us all.

Henry

"What do you think about this Nation thing, Miguel?" I say as we walk through a six-flat gangway. We're far enough away now that I stop to flare the low gray-enameled ceiling in Old English—SCR / Farwell and Clark / CSS—Slim ✟ Miguel ✟ Walter, drop the crown ☙. There's so much untagged territory here out this way.

Seems like maybe the cops don't pay too much attention to this area, so this is cool, lets me relax a lil. We can chill, do some tagging, I guess. Ain't nobody chasing us.

"'on't know, bro. How 'bout you?" Miguel says.

Walter chews the inside corner of his mouth like he always does, draws a top-hatted bunny, a cracked five-pointed star, pauses his marker figuring out what to put up next.

"Probably gonna be a good thing, I guess. As long as these mugs cover our ass like they expect us to cover theirs," I say.

Miguel laughs, a short bark. "We'll see about that, Henry."

"All we can do is hope, I guess."

"Ain't too much of that around," he sneers. "C'mon Carlito," he says to his brother, tilting his head toward the back alley, "looks good. Let's go."

Walter pops the top on his Sanford, licks his finger and wipes at a little smudge on the bunny's bow tie. We knock over a couple of stinky-ass garbage cans and truck down the alley.

TEDDY

The whiteboys would be fine; this neighborhood was full of folks that looked like them. But the rest of us, well, I all of a sudden got the feeling we'd have to step lively and light now, heads down, destination only, no stops, no convenience stores, no more tagging. Especially since it was now early after first-shift work time and some of these locals would be milling around, talking about the shit that went down over at the school, their immigrant dislike of us crackling along under the surface, looking for an excuse to boil over. C/P/W ran this neighborhood, sure, but racism is a helluva drug and those boys were all busy right now while these DPs and Polacks were getting drunker by the minute. I didn't share that with Mikey, 'cause he knew way better than I did what the consequences of angry whiteness could be.

'What you thinking about now, Midget?" Mikey asked, snapping the cap on his marker.

"Nothin'."

"Don't lie, Folks."

"I ain't lying, homes. Got any of those 100s left?"

He pulled out a raggedy-ass soft pack, handed me a Kool.

"Thanks, brother," I said, dug for my lighter.

He took one out, put the pack back in his pocket. Laid that square in the palm of his hand, the edge of the filter just past his middle finger, smacked the inside of his elbow and flipped the cigarette into his mouth. This motherfucker. I held up the Bic to his smoke. He puffed away and laughed. It got me every time.

"Damn, homes," I shook my head.

"What's up now, Teddy?" He grinned big, hands wide at his sides, blew out a huge puff of smoke around the cigarette he held in his teeth.

"You see it, homes."

"That's right," he laughed. "So, tell me what you're thinking about."

"Nothing, bro. Just sweating us all getting back home."

"Why you worry about us, Teddy?"

"It's my job, bro."

"No it ain't."

"It *is,* man."

We kept walking, moving pretty quick through this alley.

Mikey took a drag off his smoke. "Maybe," he said.

"Who else is gonna do it?" I asked.

"Fair point," he said.

"What kind of debate club shit is that to say?" I said.

"What?" he laughed. "You ain't the only one who reads books."

"Fair point," I said.

He shook his head, laughed, flicked the ash off his cigarette.

We walked on, finishing our smokes, summer light golding every surface in sight. It was warm, but not hot like earlier. We even had a steady breeze.

"Hold it right there, Injun." A serious Chicago accent crackled over a squad car PA.

Fuck. The cops had pulled through an open side yard into the alley right in front of us. Shouldn't'a been fucking around back there. I knew better, and now here we were. I kept walking, read the bullshit WE SERVE AND PROTECT in red on the side of the Chicago blue-striped, year-old white Impala, laughed to myself.

"What's so fuckin' funny," the tubby driver asked, hauling his fat ass out of the car.

"Nothin', officer. I'm just kinda simple is all."

"Is that right? What are you doing around here?" His partner got out, split us up. Damn. Police in this town rarely ever got out of their cars. Uh-oh.

"Going to the store for our grandma."

"Bullshit. Who's the shine with you?"

These fucking bigot assholes. Mikey held his hands out to his sides, hickory stick still in his hand, cocked his head while the other cop patted him down.

"My little brother," I answered.

"Is that right?"

"Yessir."

"He don't look like no Injun to me."

"Well, he is sir."

"How's that?" He looked Mikey up and down.

"He just is."

"How?"

I resisted the easy "How" joke. Said, "I don't understand the question, officer. *Simple,* remember?"

"So, you're a smart-ass Injun, then." He adjusted his utility belt or whatever that was, the fat fuck.

"No, sir. Just a simple one."

"Don't fuck with me, boy."

"I would never, officer."

"Where are you from?"

Coyote whispered in my ear—*Hit 'em with whatever language you know. That'll throw 'em off-balance, turn things your way a little.* I tilted my head, said, "Hau mitakuyepi. Cante waste nape ciyu—"

"What the fuck are you saying?" He squinted, cutting me off from my proper introduction.

". . . zapelo. Never mind, officer. I'm from around here," I said.

"Where do you live, smart guy? What's your address?"

Shit. Uh . . .

"4703 N. Bernard."

"Is that right?"

"Yessir. It is."

"Up against the car," he said. "And spread 'em."

I'd heard it so many times I assumed it was the first thing they learned in cop school and the only thing they remembered besides "don't make me shoot you," right before they tried. He kicked my feet out wide, frisked me, stopped when he got to my back left pocket.

"What the fuck is this?"

"I don't know, officer; I can't see what you're doing back there."

"Turn around, slow."

I did.

He was holding my comb.

"It's a Goody comb, officer."

He looked at it close, like he'd never seen one before. He held it by the teeth, pulled on the handle, hoping it would turn into something else.

"This it? No secret Injun shit?" he asked.

"Again, I'm not sure I understand the question, officer."

"You got no weapons, no nothing? You're on your way to the store for your grandma?"

"That's right, officer."

"What kind of shit are you buying?"

"Wójapi, manoomin, asaawe, shit like that, sir."

"Is that right, smart-ass?"

"I guess so, officer."

"I don't know what any of that crap is if you can even find it around here. You're a long way from Uptown."

I said all serious-like, "There's a secret Injun network, officer. We're everywhere, you know. Chicago has always been Indian country."

He seemed to actually pause at that, if thinking for him was signified by his lil eyebrows wiggling and his cheek just a-twitchin'. "Get the fuck outta here," he finally spit out. "And take your 'brother' with you." He air-quoted and belched. "Moran! Let him go. This Geronimo is getting on my nerves."

"Anything else I can help you with, officer?" I asked.

"Just fuck off, okay? And stay out of trouble."

"We can do that, officer." I smiled wide.

"I'm sure you can, one little Injun."

The two of them hopped back in the vehicle. The other one took Mikey's stick with him, tossed it in the backseat. Fatty threw the squad car into drive, and they peeled out, small-dick energy fading down the alley.

"Damn, bro. They didn't like you at all," Mikey said.

"Fuck the pigs," I said. "I can't believe the one made off with your hickory stick."

"Yeah, fuck the pigs," he agreed.

"Not gonna lie, bro," I said, "I was nervous as hell, and those guys were bullies, but I guess you know how to deal with bullies. Fuck 'em."

"Yup. Fuck 'em, bro." He slapped his chest.

"Fuck 'em."

"You never did tell me what you were thinking about," he said.

I fished around for my smokes, pulled the box of Reds out of my front left pocket along with my lighter. Flipped it open and held it out to Mikey, who took out two, handed one to me. I held the light out for him, then me, said, "That shit right back there, actually. How the fuckin' cops are the worst gang to have to go up against. They're a bunch of immoral fucks with better equipment than us. And hard-ons for anyone who ain't white." I blew out a big drag, put the smokes away, and ran my hands through my hair, stopping to scratch my scalp along the way, cigarette hanging from the side of my mouth.

"That's weird, bro, but I believe you," he said.

"What do you mean?"

"I mean of course you're thinking about some shit like that." He laughed.

I did, too. "Well, what were you thinking about?" I said.

"Trying to hook up with Juanita, homes."

"Dang, bro. You've been at that for a while now." We crossed Sunnyside, stuck to the alley.

"She digs me, man!"

"Sure, homes."

"For real." He raised his eyebrows as high as they would go, grinned just small.

"Okay."

"On the Nation, Folks."

Well, that was serious.

"Alright, Folks. I believe you."

"Damn straight, Teddy. You better."

"I do, bro, I do." I repped an R over my chest.

"Alright, then," he said, repped it back.

"Alright."

We walked. I could hear and smell folks starting to make dinner and whatnot, boiled potatoes, backyard grills, and kids getting shushed. *So* Ozzie and Harriet. This neighborhood was wild and dull all at once.

"Mikey, man. What did you think of all that back at the schoolyard?" I said.

"Those Gaylords? They can't shoot for shit."

"Nah. I mean true, but not that."

"Little Man and them getting busted by the cops?"

"Nope."

"The three hundred Royals on the blacktop?"

"No. The speeches and all," I said.

"You gotta not do this shit, Midget," he sighed. "We can't read your fuckin' mind. All the stuff in that big old head of yours. Always thinking and expecting us to know what about. It ain't right. Don't be so fuckin' . . . vague and teachery all the time, like we're having a quiz or some shit. No wonder the cops call you Professor."

"My bad. Sorry, bro." He was right.

"It's okay. But yeah, fuck a speech. What are we, Romans or some?"

"True, true. I feel you, bro. Probably could've just had the prezzes and warlords meet and let everyone know what's up later. That shit was dull as fuck, Folks. We were supposed to get fired up, but

I faded big-time when we started hearing about dues and reporting and whatnot. That's probably necessary in the joint and all, but out here in the world we gotta worry about getting moved on and protecting our territory. How we're gonna get our folks fed and taken care of, feel?" I thought about what Coyote had talked about when it came to community and whatnot.

"Yeah," he said, "but you know what? I think they wanted folks to be impressed, see some numbers, see what the fuck we can do."

"You're right about that, homes," I said. "And shit *was* impressive. But so what?"

"I hear you," he said. "But yeah, did you know we had those kind of numbers?"

"Not like that, bro," I said. "I guessed we were doing okay, but not *that* good, no."

"Kinda dramatic, though. A little bit Warriors, right?" He rolled his eyes.

"Yeah, but it's okay, I guess. A touch of flash can't hurt, right?" I flicked my smoke.

"It can if the brothers think all kinds of Folks got their back out there and that ain't how it's gonna be." He threw his smoke back over his shoulder, ran a hand over his head.

"Truth. This Nation thing better be for real. If I'm getting down with some Unknowns in my old hood those Latin Eagles needa step up," I said.

"See? You think that shit's gonna happen? We been going at it with those motherfuckers for a long time now. Then we're supposed to be cool with them? Back 'em up? I ain't really feeling it, Folks."

"We'll find out, I suppose."

"Better hope it don't cost your life on the show." He grinned.

"I'll check it on the turn, brother."

"I bet you will."

"You know it, homes."

Mikey

Teddy is fucking crazy if he thinks this whole Nation thing is gonna work out. I don't understand his optimism. I mean for real; I appreciate it, and it gives the boys something to hang on to, but still, man. The only Folks that got your back is your folks, know what I'm sayin'? But yeah, maybe we can ride this shit for a minute. We might get a few years out of it. We should probably get on it for what it's worth every day, but I still ain't sure. I'll be taking care of my business and my own homies every minute. Latin Eagles? Imperial Gangsters? Man, fuck those guys. We'll see what happens. Bet. When the shit goes down, they'll leave us hanging, every time. But as long as we know that we'll be alright. We're gonna need to talk about it. I know Teddy'll want to, 'cause if he ain't one hundred percent then something ain't right. If we jump up with this Nation business, things'll get really real. And I don't think the fellas are ready for all that's gonna bring. I know it, and so does he. But right now ain't the time to bring it up.

For real, though, homes, we haven't eaten all day. I'm starvin' like Marvin. Hope the old lady brings home something good tonight. And not some fuckin' frog legs like the other day. Shit was nasty. Who the fuck eats those? This is the North. We don't have to eat that stuff. We got some weird motherfuckers in this town. I thought about Juanita, maybe take her out for a gyro or something instead of some leftovers from the fridge.

Teddy

The alley dead-ended behind the buildings that faced onto Montrose. We hooked left, heading toward our planned meetup on

Kedzie. We crossed Christiana, stuck with the alley route. I didn't want to be on the main avenue until the last possible minute. I thought there might be Kings over this way. Montrose was always Latin Kings for me; there was a branch down by my old, old neighborhood where it crossed Hazel, so in my mind there'd be Kings here, too. There might be Imperial Gangsters ♚ or something, but I didn't want to test the full Nationhood quite yet. Besides, I didn't see any of their reps at the meeting, so even though we were all Folks, this wasn't the place to count on their loyalty to something so new. We were way too far from home. And if this hood wasn't I ♚ G, it was probably Gaylords ✠. Those weaselly whiteboys popped up everywhere, it seemed, and if they were gonna be anywhere, it was out here in Albany Park, the last white ethnic stronghold on the city's North Side.

Chicago was a funny place, the most segregated big city in the country. But it wasn't so much a city as it was a collection of neighborhoods and villages. But for being segregated, it was probably the most diverse place in America as a whole. Food-wise, we had everything, sure, but there were Mexican restaurants that served dishes only available here and in the village the chef was from. We had such deep connections to soul food and the South that when mighty El Rukn leader Jeff Fort, legendary negotiator of missile deals with Muammar Gaddafi, escaped, even I was like, "Well, just check Mississippi, yeah?" Sure enough, there he was. Anyway, we got Colombian seafood joints, Haitian cuisine, Lebanese halal, and Greek spots on almost every corner that'll make you gyros and eggs on request down the street from hillbilly joints that crank out jelly omelets and fried bologna along with Michelin-starred French restaurants that make mayors cry over foie gras ordinances and Maxwell Street Polishes that should be bronzed and more famous than that deep-dish special occasion pizza the rest of the country thinks we eat every damn day. Talk all the shit you want about New York or Portland, but you can eat your way through two dozen countries on a Sunday Clark Street stroll. Shit, we even have multiple *Swedish* restaurants. Fuck you.

I was getting hungry. Can you tell?

"What's for supper, bro?" I asked.

"Whut?"

"I don't know. I'm hungry, I guess. Just thinking about food."

"Man, I don't know. Whatever my ma brings home, I suppose. What about you?"

Mikey's ma was a waitress. So was mine. And Mikey2 and 3's both. A couple more from the crew, too, now that I thought about it. Sometimes they brought home leftovers. When I still lived with my ma, she would bring home Gullivers, the best deep dish in the city for real. But that was only once in a while. Usually, it was white bread with margarine and garlic salt in the broiler. I used to watch my little brother and sisters while she was at work. Garlic bread and Kool-Aid was supper unless I went to the National's and stole tortillas to throw on the burners for some variety.

"Sometimes the old man comes home and passes out, sometimes we go out to eat," I said.

"For real? That's pretty cool."

It was, too. I still love to go out to eat. Such a luxury.

"Yeah. Depends how fucked-up he is. Toward the end of the week, forget it, but it's Tuesday, right? So, who knows?" I crossed my fingers in my pants pocket.

"Right on, brother. Good thoughts. Man, I'd love to go out to eat," he said.

"We'll get there, homes. Do some bottles tomorrow, or maybe a little job out on the far side of the hood by Indian Boundary, get some cash. Go to the Gold Coin or some."

"It's a deal, brother." He beamed.

Fuck. I really wished we'd brought the boom box.

MIKEY

We pop out onto Kedzie Avenue, swing right toward Montrose.

Hector and Bugs are wrestling on the corner; Pepper looking up and down the street, his perpetually dumbass open-mouthed stare wide enough I can see his fillings from here; Mikey2 and 3 are leaning against the eastbound bus stop hut, bored, while Lil Demon and Psycho stroll up close, telling each other crazy stories of whatever the fuck goes through their heads; Lil Capone is whipping his head back and forth like it was Belfast or something, sending up smoke to Jesus in hopes it wasn't. The rest of the set clomps along about a half block away, a few crossing the middle of the street over to the south side, cars honking at them. There isn't a bus in sight, so no hurry.

"Lookit this shit, bro," I say, suddenly full of pride for our set.

"What?" Teddy sticks out his chin. "That?"

"All these Royals chilling in enemy territory. Pretty cool." Maybe this Nation thing could work out.

"Bolo, how you know this is opposition turf? Man, you're paranoid." It seems like he was fucking with me.

"I ain't."

"You see enemies everywhere, homes."

"Just like you," I say.

"Do you know who runs this joint? Are you clocking the tags?" he says.

"No. That's your job."

"Exactly, Folks. So don't be criticizing."

The best way to make a bus come is to light a cigarette, so I do. "You want one of these?" I ask.

"Nah, I'm good," he says.

Man. Dude never turns down a smoke. First time for everything, I guess. It had been one of those days. "Alright, Folks," I say. "Suit yourself."

I look at all four corners. There's a sky-blue Freak tag on the side of the Buy Low liquor store, but it has to be at least three years old; no worries there. Maybe he's right.

We are about to cross the street. The boys haven't seen us yet.

TEDDY

"Gaylords! Royal Killer!"

I laughed. Everybody jumped.

"What's up, Folks? Royal!" Hector hollered.

Psycho reached for his empty pistol, saw it was us, grinned, and turned it into a back scratch. Lil Demon looked at him questioningly, then knowingly, beamed too, up-nodded.

Pepper gulped, finally closed his mouth for a minute. Everyone relaxed.

We crossed over to the bus stop, everyone shaking hands in reunion.

There was a panadería right off the corner. They must've just pulled a batch of something from the oven. The smell was driving me crazy. I lit a smoke to ward off hunger.

"Alright, Folks. We ready to get the fuck out of here?"

"Hell yeah," three or four of them said.

"Same, Folks, same," I said. "Guess we'll have to take the bus. Everyone got those tokens still? Alright. Make sure you get a transfer so we can take the El where it finally meets up with Montrose here. Y'all got dimes for transfers, right?"

"Yeah. We're good, Folks," a bunch of them said.

I couldn't believe we all made it. Well, almost made it. Our connection to the El was a full fourteen blocks away. We'd have to get all the way to Honore without any incidents. I crossed my fingers again, made sure no one was looking, rolled the tobacco from a Red out onto the street.

We chilled, told stories, laughed, built up our tales to tell for later.

My smoke was about halfway cashed so I stepped out into the street and sure enough, the bus was two blocks away.

"Bus coming, Folks," I said.

A couple of the fellas looked up, looked down at their smokes, cussed a little.

"Get ready to put 'em out boys. We're fixing to go home," I said.

A carload cruised by, slow, westbound on Montrose. A pale green '67 Biscayne. I made them for Kings, but they might've been IGs. Who knows?

Anyway.

"Coronas, boys," I said, just loud enough for us but not them to hear.

They scoped us. We were nineteen strong, and it looked like they stopped counting at eight, drove on.

"Power in numbers, Folks," I laughed.

"Damn, bro," Henry said.

"Feels good, don't it, homes," I said.

"For real, brother, it does," Walter popped in.

"This Nation stands, Folks, and it'll be like that all the time," I said.

"I ain't holding my breath, Teddy," Miguel said.

"I ain't either, Miguel," I replied, "but I'ma hope for the best. Those could've been Imperial Gangsters who didn't cap us, homes. We don't know this hood at all." I switched it up, tried to show them the best possible scenario. For some reason I suddenly wanted this Nation to really be a thing in the world.

It would keep the peace a bit, I thought. I mean, yeah, in some neighborhoods you'd be instantly at war, but at least you knew that going into it as long as you knew your business and who was who. Shit used to be all kinda chaos. This way it would be easier to keep track of things. And it would be nice to know where the last of the white whiteboys stood.

"Maybe, bro. We'll see." That was probably the most I'd heard Miguel say in the last year. His brother talked even less. Man, me and Walter had won a half dozen foosball tournaments together and exchanged maybe five words outside of "good job" and "we'll split the pot," and I considered him a friend and brother. But yeah. My old man was the same way, so fine, I guess. What a day.

The bus roared in, diesel exhaust billowing over us and air-brake pressure wailing in our eardrums. We trudged up the narrow stairs, paid our fares, got transfers for the El. There were only a couple people on board. We rolled to the back, filled up the seats. The sky was gray and talked plenty of shit about rain we knew wasn't coming. I smelled the ozone, but I knew better. Late summer / early fall Chicago pulled this shit all the time. The cielo said tornado, but we knew better. Lots of wind and bluster, green clouds and angry air, but all it would do is get hotter and more humid. We opened every window wide, hung way out loud, talked shit to people on the street. Anything could happen, sure, but it would probably happen in our favor. I still couldn't believe the driver was cool with all nineteen of us getting on together. I tried to be friendly, but still. He laughed nervous every now and again, ate his donuts, drank his coffee, and sailed east, his bus full of gangbangers enjoying the sights and sounds of the Northwest Side on a tour he never thought he'd be leading.

Myself, I took the seat all the way in the back right corner and settled in, me and the *Boss* riding all the way back toward the neighborhood, window wide open, warm wind howling in, and me in love with everything we could ever be.

My bazillionth read of the Back of the Yards section must've dragged or else I was beat from all the shit that went down, 'cause I fell asleep at some point. I woke up right before Western Avenue, whipped my eyes but not my head around. The fellas were chillin', smoking cigarettes out the windows, nothing crazy happening. The bus was empty except for us.

"Alright, boys. Stop's coming up in a minute."

"Yeah, yeah," they laughed and hollered back. "We got you, Folks."

These were some good brothers, no doubt. I couldn't believe I fell asleep. RJ was in lockup, so I knew no one would've drawn a dick on my face or whatnot.

Mikey said, "You were snoring, bro. You alright?"

"Yeah, man. I'm good."

"Alright, Folks," he laughed.

MiKEY

It's wild. Teddy has this thing where he can just fall asleep if he's tired. In the park, the alley, wherever, I'll look over and that mothe-fucker will be out. Dude's head must've been cooking so much that he needs to recharge or whatever, and that's it, he's asleep. And my brother snores, so no way to hide it. Just gone. But for only like five minutes and then he'll be twice as awake as before, on fire and ready to go. Dang. The problem, though, is he'll wake up with some crazy new idea he'd want to do right away, and I'll be like, bro, that's just some dreamtime shit and he'll be all "if you don't listen to your dreams you'll die, you'll fuck it all up," and off we'll go on some wild mission stealing from the Jewel's or moving out on some Assyrian Eagles because we have to listen to his dreams. It's like he can see a future none of us can. It doesn't happen a lot, but still, when it does, it's a pain in the ass. I think, "Who lives their life like this," but I always have an answer—he does—and we have to go along with it. I figure it's some Injun shit, but still. It usually works out, though not always. But on a betting scale it's better than fifty-fifty, so why not go with it?

TEDDY

The El station was right up ahead; it pitched closer through the big front windows of the bus; the tops of the enameled white stanchions blazed gold with the fire of the sun angling ever lower behind us. I hung near the front door, standing in the aisle, holding the overhead railing. The bus driver poked along down Montrose, letting every car in and out of parking spots. It was maddening, felt like all those drivers laughed with the knowledge that a train was about to pull in and we needed to be on it bad, couldn't afford to hang out on the platform in this unknown neighborhood. I didn't have a license, but I'd seen a few and preferred to imagine right now that Illinois secretary of state Alan J. Dixon's motto told all the holders to drive "like an asshole," instead of "defensively." Our own driver sensed we were getting antsy, all nineteen of us, not an angry number he wanted to think too much about. He stopped fucking around and stepped on the gas, let us out under the viaduct with the southbound train about two blocks away.

"Alright, boys, let's get it," I said loud, heading down the stairs at the front exit, half of us heading that way, the others out the back door so we'd all make it on time. "Everyone got their transfers? Get 'em out and let's make this smooth. The train's almost here." Folks grumbled and whatnot, but pretty much everyone seemed ready to get back to the El, to the last part of this trip. Chill on the train, transfer to the Jackson Park–Englewood line, and go the fuck home.

Getting through the station was quick; after the first few of our transfers checked out, the agent waved the rest of us through. A couple of the fellas made eyes at the little newsstand like they wanted to buy some chips or candies or whatever, but I quashed that shit. "Let's go! Train's almost here!" I heard the screech of the lead car grinding the rust off the rails as we started to hit the stairs heading up to the platform, smelled the electric arcs jumping in the late summer sun. "Hustle up, Folks," I said, taking the stairs two at a time.

The platform popped up quick and I jogged down about fifteen feet, stood next to one of the movie billboards on the partition wall. Clint glared at me from a hole in the wall at Alcatraz, then hovered over my shoulder and helped me count heads coming up the stairs. We were all here as the train pulled in, cool. It was a little crowded this time of day with college students heading to night classes at DePaul and lame reverse commuters on their way to rapidly gentrifying Lincoln Park. We found seats where we could, made people nervous, and thought about the day we just had. It wasn't too far to our transfer spot at Belmont so I kept the book in my pocket, looked out the window. Four or five stops to go ain't worth the break I'd have to make in reading.

Instead, I decided to take notes on the folks in the car, using fancy book-style. I watched a couple of blond-streaked Beccas on their way to a comparative religion class; so edgy. Their parents would be pissed—"What are those Vincentians teaching you? I thought it was a good Catholic school!" I saw their professor doing his prep for tonight's class. He wore an argyle sweater vest and a pair of Walgreens reading glasses. It was like he wanted people to know who he was and what he was about. His loneliness fluttered unheeded into the air with every flip of the page. He'd been working on a book for fifteen years that his mother would ask him about at holiday dinners. His pissy attitude let her know that genuine scholarship takes time. He'll never finish it but told himself he will when he retires. And he'll drop dead from sadness and rejection before he can even write his unappreciated and unread acknowledgments.

A petty businessman shuffled papers from a cheap briefcase. His boss didn't know who he was and cared even less about his ideas. He'll pick up a Hungry-Man fried chicken, mashed potatoes, and corn TV dinner from the Jewel's on his way home, watch *Happy Days* and *Laverne & Shirley,* then pass out in his recliner. At 11 p.m. he'll roll out of the BarcaLounger, take a shower, get in his unmade bed, and dream about splitting his boss's head open with the office fire extinguisher. He'll wake up in a sweat that will startle him with its coolness, take fright at the heat of his dream, and recoil at the horror of the violence it presented him with, even as he holds it dear during his dreary workday, a routine he'll trudge to for thirty more years, watching six more bosses advance to national spots in the company, visions of their shattered heads marching out the door of his eternally regional office. He'll never marry, and his modest estate will be bickered over by his ungrateful brother and penniless sisters.

We were coming up to the Southport stop. I scanned the platform. This was usually neutral territory and appeared it would remain that way today. We picked up a few passengers and moved on down the line. I relaxed in my seat as the doors closed, the conductor announcing way too close in the mic for the overhead PA system that the next stop would be Belmont, change for Jackson Park, Englewood, and Evanston Express trains. Still, his heavy voice couldn't mask "Superstition" coming out of the little radio he kept in the cab.

Hey, there was the twenty-four-year-old ethnic white guy who'll win the forty-four-million-dollar lottery in a few years and think about buying a bowling alley. He took a window seat, scratched his big Slavic mustache, and settled in, staring out the big glass.

I looked to see what he was seeing, pulled out my black magnum and tagged the wall under the window, never taking my eyes off our mutual horizon, the fumes drifting up slow and sweet. It was mostly trees whipping by; a last splash of golding greenery before we made the turn into the deeper city, all buildings and concrete from here on out.

Two silver-almost-purple-haired old ladies in beautiful bright print dresses, survivors of Auschwitz with Zs before the numbers tattooed on their arms, laughed and huddled close, their heads almost touching. They held their big bags full of Romani old-lady things on their thin laps and smiled at me when they noticed me looking their way. I smiled back, unable to imagine the things they'd seen, waved my fingers at them. They went back to laughing in a way that made me feel finer than I had all day.

Whoa. There was a Native dude who looked like Coyote. "Sungmanitu," I said under my breath, "why are you here?" He was walnut brown and wiry, wearing a pair of mirrored Aviators; old, faded jeans and a white T-shirt with the sleeves cut off; ratty black high-top Chucks with washed-out royal blue laces. He had long black hair parted down the middle and this little thin mustache with a couple of chin hairs. Looked Cree or maybe Ojibwe. Could've been Lakota, too, but Coyote tends to hum in and out of focus, so though I couldn't really tell where he was from, my day got better anyway. It was rare to see a cousin out and about, so even if it was Coyote and that meant anything could happen, it was worth it. I looked around my seat for Iktómi just in case, 'cause that would've been a lot, but we were all clear. I tapped each of my four fingers on my thumb, pulled out a cigarette, split the spine with my right thumbnail, poured the tobacco into the palm of my left hand, held it to my heart like I'd see in a movie in a few years, said a prayer, and starting at the pinkie, rolled my fingers open like a wing, poured it all out on the floor of the car between my legs, watching it drop. I looked up to see Coyote grinning at me nice and big. I cut my eyes to the window quick, catching the last of the big maples at the turn, chunks of leaves at the top already fading to rose and gold, said another prayer.

Of course, since Coyote was on our train the platform at Belmont was engulfed in flames, mostly clear now with just a few folks running for the exits down to the stairs. Jesusfuckingchrist. I snuck a look at him, but he was crackling in and out of my vision. I figured I was the only one who could see him anyway, so fuck it, I wasn't gonna ask anyone else if he was really there; besides, they were all glued to the windows watching the inferno on the platform. Coyote snapped back into the car mostly full-on, but still a little fuzzy, standing now, leered and walked over to the doors, tried to pull the emergency stop.

Because he was only nominally on this plane, it didn't work, and we sailed through the Belmont stop. The conductor breathed heavy into the PA, voice an octave higher, told us the next stop would be Fullerton. Coyote grinned even bigger, winked out of sight, a pale bright blue twist of smoke the only thing announcing his existence and exit.

I leaned in close to the mostly bulletproof glass, saw flames running up the front of the station, planks by the stairs on fire, the big cardboard advertisements shooting hot red and orange up over the lips of the overhangs that nominally protected passengers from rain but in no way covered their asses when snow whipped off the lake from the east or roared across the prairies to the west. It was hard to hide from the weather in Chicago. The city made half-hearted investments in doing so, but after 150 years or so in business, they knew protests were futile. The

heating lamps and shades at bus and El stops were cute commit-
ments, but mostly decorative. It's okay, though, we were all in
on the joke.

MIKEY

Holy shit, bro, the whole station is on fire. What the fuck, yo. I
clock Teddy just chillin', looking at some spot out the window
like everything is normal. The conductor is talking into the mic
like this shit happened every day. It feels like we're accelerating
through the platform full speed down the line. Makes sense, I
guess. Don't really want to stop in the middle of a fire. The next
Ravenswood stop is Wellington and then Diversey, but this cat
doesn't give a shit about that, I guess—says we were headed to
Fullerton, Jackson-Englewood all the way. Maybe because we've
been hauling ass and the station comes up so quick after we make
the turn onto the Englewood line he can't stop in time. Or maybe
he's a gangbanger, too, and knows some shit we don't. At any rate,
nothing feels right about this; it seems like someone somewhere lit
this shit on fire. It would be good to know who that was. I have a
funny feeling about pulling into the next station. I laugh, 'cause if
it was the Orphans like in the movie, we'd be having a good time.
But this ain't Hollywood and the only thing I can do about it is
to be ready, I guess.

HENRY

Crazy, man. The platform is blazing, and the set is nervous. How
the fuck did this even happen? Was it a lightning strike? It's shitty
out like it's gonna rain, but this is nuts. The sky went from kinda

sunny to green in a couple of minutes. Anyway, it sounds like we're gonna push right on through to Fullerton. I wonder if those Unknowns are still hanging around. The shit part is if they are, they'll have all kinds of backup now. They weren't a big set from what I could tell, but if they call up their Insane Deuce buddies, we'll be in a world of hurt, for sure.

PEPPER

Some fuckin' commotion right here for real. There's a fire, Lord knows where it's coming from or how it got started, but gonna be some opportunity here no doubt. Maybe those Unknowns'll be there at Fullerton, and Teddy'll get his ass kicked good. That'd be nice. I might even be able to help that situation along. I've had enough of his shit to last me a couple lifetimes. Hector'll take care of business for our set, I ain't worried. Me, I'm nipping on this whiskey and settling in to see how shit goes down. Cain't wait.

LIL DEMON

Just wild, bro. Hahaha. Like being on Great America's best ride ever. We cruise through the station, shit on fire, mugs yelling, sirens blazing, and this conductor just "blahblahblah" on the mic like nothing, all casual, might as well be saying "keep your arms and legs inside the ride," et cetera and all. I'm still buzzing a little from that gunfight at the schoolyard. Tried to tag those GLs in their old beater, but I couldn't get there fast enough. I needa unleash on somebody. I jump out of my seat. Let's be ready, Folks.

TEDDY

For all the calm old boy been having on the intercom he sure got dramatic when we hit the platform at Fullerton. Must've been some supervisors hanging out 'cause he went from casual mumbling to textbook clarity and diction in about two seconds flat, backing out safe exit instructions and procedures like a promotion depended on it. I needed a landmark for us to meet up at and picked this tacky lime-green and navy-blue fake-ass vintage ad for a bank.

We rolled into the station like it was a CTA training exercise, followed some orderly directives, and spilled out onto the platform. I looked around at the crew; folks were on high alert and amped up. Lawsuits were holding their necks and feigning trauma all over the car. The city was gonna be paying out on this one.

"Meet up by the First Chicago sign, Folks!" I yelled into the chaos, stepped off the train.

LIL PSYCHO

Man, my clip is empty, and I have a bad feeling about this shit. I didn't pack anything else, figured the piece would be enough if any shit went down, but now I wish I would've. This is a funky neighborhood, and I never really come down this way. After the shit we'd done to those Unknowns on our way out to Roosevelt, I'm a little worried they might be hanging out waiting to pay us back.

Sure enough, I can see that Lil Ghost dude up on top of the crossover. I look around and there's the rest of the set, even that

Young Lover dude hobbling down the steps toward the platform where we are about to pull in. Shit. I pull the pistol out of the back of my waistband, hold it under my shirt. Maybe flashing it will be enough. We pull into the station.

TEDDY

We never made it to the stupid billboard. A mess of Unknowns and three or four Deuces were waiting for us when we walked off the car. Goddamnit, I hated these motherfuckers, too, especially since they killed Arab back in the day. Also, they mostly ran the Horseshoe Projects, officially called the Lathrop Homes, where my grandparents and uncle lived. No way I could ever visit those two. Fuck. So here we had a set that prevented me from seeing my family *and* killed the president of our set, a dude who looked like us, talked like us, thought about us in the midst of tall white nonsense. Fuck you. It's on.

"There's a bunch of Deuces here, too, Folks!" I hollered.

I wished Lil Psycho had a few rounds left in that .22 of his 'cause I would've emptied it into this rat king of fuckheads. I wished RJ was here right now, too. I reached into my right front pocket, slipped my middle finger through the two end rings on three feet of dog chain, pulled it out slow, and quick backhanded Lil Ghost with it on the bridge of his nose. I watched his pretty, perfect skin split in slow motion but wasn't quick enough to dodge the blood spray that misted my shades when everything went back to full speed. Fuck. That's okay. I'll clean it up later. Ghost slumped on the platform holding his face with both hands, rocking back and forth making weird sounds. We whaled into the pile.

MIKEY

Young Lover. What the fuck kind of a name is that? Innyway, this is the cat that Hector threw off the platform earlier. Gotta give it up, though, Folks. This mug is coming for more, limping our way. Should feel a lil bad about fuckin' his crippled ass up, but he's about it, so here we go.

This thing happens when you humbug. It's wild, and I cain't figure out how it happens, but you . . . isolate, like in Bruce Lee movies. You know how you ask, "How the fuck are they fighting one at a time?" Well, yeah. It's like that, that's what they're trying to capture. It happens for real. Time slows down and it's like there's a camera or something, just you and the dude you're squaring up with. That was happening now with this Young Lover cat. It's so cool when that kicks in, 'cause you got all kinds of time to decide what you're gonna do. Example, you're never supposed to lead with an uppercut, but this looked a chance to try it. Yup. That shit landed like in the movies. Old boy went down like his legs got cut off. I know it ain't easy to knock a motherfucker out, but dang. I got some lucky today.

I laugh and hope I can do it again.

LIL DEMON

Goddamn it's about time. Didn't get to do shit back at the school-yard, but right now we have a whole pile of opposition up close and personal-like, so we get to do some damage. I know we were supposed to be skins, and I might get a violation for packing, but there's no way I was heading that far from our hood without some protection. My big brother bought me this knife before he went away for a ten piece on a manslaughter charge he pled out to, his shitty public defender too lazy to argue self-defense when he killed a King with a lawn chair down at the lake after the guy pulled a pistol on him. There were three other Coronas that would've killed him for sure if they weren't so freaked out after the bent aluminum tubing tore open the dude's jugular. That was some messy shit to have happen when we were just trying to barbecue on the beach. He got a helluva rep and a way-too-long stretch out of it. I'd be an old man by the time he got out, but today his gift to me was gonna sing.

There are some cats on the platform in front of us that aren't the same dudes as earlier. Teddy is yelling about Deuces when we're getting off the train, and I know those were the fuckers that killed Arab so there's about to be some payback. I reach down into my sock and pull out the knife my brother gave me, hit the button, and hear the blade snick out. There are two dudes squaring up, so I pick the one on the right and duck down like I was going for his legs. When he tilts his head down to meet my grab I reach up and stab him in the face, just miss his eye. You take out someone's eye in any way and you don't really have to worry about them for the rest of the fight. The point went in right under his socket, so I twist up, try to find the sweet spot, but he pulls away quick. Dangit. I slash at his partner's larynx, miss, feel the edge dig into his shoulder, the blade bunching up in his black T-shirt. Shit. I hold on to the handle tighter so I don't lose my weapon. He pulls away and I still have my knife. Then both of these fools take off running, the one dude holding his face, the other grabbing at his shoulder. Not good enough. Somebody else is gonna get stabbed good and proper. I look around for my next dance. Walter and Miguel have their hands full, so I hustle their way.

HECTOR

Alright. This shit is live, homes. All kinds of opposition here, Deuces and Unknowns, take your pick. Here comes that Lil Ghost dude again. Damn, this punk is a hardhead. Never learns. That's alright. I'm about to become a professor myself.

Hahaha. Dang. Teddy pulls a chain out of his pocket and whacks that fucker across the nose. Messssy. Clean up on aisle nine and shit. Fuck. Dropped him to the ground. No worries, though. We ain't done. Mikey drops that Young Lover cat and I stomp his face then hustle up, give Teddy a head nod and one-hand Ghost by the neck over to the edge of the platform. I grab him by the ass with my other hand and toss him over. He lands just right. I hear a little sizzle sound and then a big pop! and it smells like when a hot dog falls through onto the coals. I look up at the little tower thing by the overpass. Three or four suits stare back at me. I smile and wave, run up the stairs toward them, figuring I'll cross over to the other side. I think I see a couple more of these Unknowns on the east side platform anyway.

WALTER AND MIGUEL

Man, these Deuces are frontin' heavy, crowding around like they're gonna do something. We don't have much beef with these cats except they're the ones who killed Arab and fuck 'em innyway if they're down with the crown like we'd heard. Have to roundhouse this one dude who pops up talking shit. He goes down and his buddies back off a bit. Well, yeah, that's just an invitation to do some mayhem and whatnot. A forearm shiv takes down another one and a stomp to his shin snaps that shit in half. It makes that sound like when you crack a chicken bone for the marrow. Lil Demon dead runs in with his brother's switch held low, gets one of them in the face. He yanks up on it, pulls it out and tries to slash another dude's throat and the rest of their boys second-guess getting down in this dance. It's wild to watch it crawl over their faces right before they book, running for the downstairs exit. We laugh, light smokes, take in the action up and down the platform. Some of the whiteboys are huddled up by the overpass. Maybe we can go check that out.

HENRY

I despise this shit and love it at the same time. A lil bit of me hates scrapping with brothers, but opposition is opposition. People make their choices and they gotta stick with 'em. These Unknown motherfuckers chose poorly, in my estimation. And now they're fixin' to pay. Some motherfucker is hollering and whatnot, coming my way. I think his name is Bashful, a light-skinned brother. He comes at me on a dead run. I lower my right shoulder into his hip and flip him over my back. He lands hard and I turn and drop on my elbow into his chest. All his air rushes out and I grab him by the hair, smack his head into the deck three or four times, quick-like. He reaches for my throat, so I pull him close, headbutt him. He starts to pass out and I help him on his way with a right to the forehead and a left to the temple. He's gonna be bashful for a while. I see Hector throw that Ghost dude onto the tracks. I think about doing this cat the same way but figure it wouldn't be cool. No need to catch a murder 1 from some bullshit humbug. Time speeds back up and I look around to see who needs a hand.

PEPPER

About to get my shot. Whole lotta chaos and whatnot going on here. I take a big hit of Earl Settler from my flask. Looks like Teddy got lucky and laid open some dude's face. Hector dragged the guy over to the third rail, so shit was fixin' to get nuts and folks are all looking over that way. I run up making like I was gonna help with my daddy's Barlow knife held wide in my right hand but for real Teddy is gonna get stabbed in the neck, oof oof oof, prison-style. He has four or five opposition around him; none of our Folks will see me in all this static and that will be the end of his shit. And if those People see me, well, they wouldn't say shit no way, 'cause they know same as I did that this fucker needs to *go*.

And then right as I'm closing on him, I trip over nothing, like someone stuck a leg out from nowhere. As I fall toward the deck, my back on fire, I reach out with my blade. It sticks good, but in his arm, drags deep as I go down.

Fuck.

Missed.

TEDDY

It got quiet like it never got quiet. No shrieking wheels on the tracks, no intercom, no express trains thundering through the station. We could see smoke rising up from the platform at Belmont, smell the creosote on the wind. I felt this deep burning in the middle of where I had to cut out that infected cross tattoo last summer, knew Pepper fragged me before I even turned, knew he thought no one was looking, got me in the arm, couldn't even stab me proper, the fucking coward. Still, it was deep, and blood leaked out of my forearm like an evening star's glow crawling over a thin maroon horizon. Outside my body and deeply in it at the same time, I watched it seep up in the pre–magic hour light canting around the edge of the big post office building, the gold embedded in the sun's rays lending flames to my deep red essence that rose to meet the fire from above. That shit hurt, no lie.

Weird, though. He had kinda fallen into me, all awkward-like. He tripped or something when he was coming at me, the shitweasel. I'm pretty sure he would've had a clear shot at me, but he went ass over teakettle at the last minute.

But for real right now if I get lockjaw from his dirty redneck knife, I'm killing this fucker's whole family. I'll burn down his apartment then catch a bus to Kentucky or whatever, take out his grandma and grandpa, too. Plus, all forty of his cousins in their knotty pine homestead.

Goddamnit.

CTA Supervisor #2134

Holy shit. Some guy that looks like, I don't know how to explain it, but like if a coyote was a person, all the sudden *appears* on the platform and trips a redheaded greaser who is about to stab this little longhair Indian kid in the big fight down below. He . . . vibrates in, does his thing, and pulses back out. The hillbilly goes down, and I watch a bright red bloom spread bright on his white dago T across his lower back, even though no weapon touches him. I can't put that in a report. Nope. No one is gonna believe this.

Other than being called to the scene of a fire at the Belmont platform, where we are tasked to monitor the overflow and subsequent routing of southbound units to the Fullerton station, this was an otherwise normal day. Well, okay, maybe a little special. I sweet-talked Marie and got her to get the cook to fix me a pepper-and-egg sandwich at Herm's even though it was a Tuesday and not a Friday, but other than that, an ordinary workday. Definitely not special enough to try pushing through some magical bullshit like this. My boss will shitcan me for sure if I turned in a writeup of what I'm seeing. I slow spin around to one of the other supervisors like, "Did you see that?" but she shakes her head, taps her pen on her lip, and goes back to acting like this is just another little incident that happens every other day.

Mikey

Shiiiit. Pepper is fixing to stab Teddy. Fuck. That redneck sonofabitch. I hustle over his way, but I'm not gonna make it. Fuck.

And then, I'll be damned. Out of nowhere this coyote-looking dude appears and fucks Pepper's shit *up*. Trips him and then dang, swipes his paw across his back and redneck blood starts running all over the place. Holy shit. That boy could die.

Wild.

I slow my roll, watch the show. Coyote guy popped out like he'd never been there at all.

Damn. Yup. Pepper was fixin' to die. And I don't feel bad about that shit.

At all.

I hurry over to where him and Teddy are all tangled up.

Lil Psycho

A clear path to the pedestrian walkway opens in the madness, a place to get a breather and assess what's happening. We group up over there, take stock of our situation. A couple of Peewee Unknowns spot us and run our way. They pull up quick when the chrome flashes on the .22, but turn and run straight into Miguel and Walter. One takes Walter's elbow straight to the mouth; two front teeth splash onto the deck in a spit of blood. Miguel throws up one of his roundhouses, connects with the side of the other one's neck. He staggers but doesn't fall, yanks his buddy away from trying to grab up his lost incisors and they run for the stairs, take them down two at a time.

Mikey2 is flushing seafoam green, ready to puke, and Mikey3's eyes are doing that vibrating thing. This seems like an exceptionally good time to get the fuck out of here. I grab Lil Capone, add 2 plus 3, and we scramble for the stairs ourselves.

Lil Demon

Damn. Carlito and Miguel have it all cleaned up by the time I get over their way. These Unknowns are kinda soft. Teddy seemed a little freaked out but now it looks like it was just a numbers game. I get it if it was just him against a few of these cats, but when the numbers even up a little bit we get right over. After the hurt we just put on them it's gonna be a minute before anybody has to worry about their shit. Too bad we run out of mugs to fuck up. Miguel and Walter scattered the Deuces, so now it's about getting out of here without getting popped. We've been getting lucky so far, but I figure a full load of cops will be here any minute. I better see about how we're gonna pull up outta this joint. Time to make a plan and hope God is still on our side.

Sure enough, I knew I should go to church more often. I look up and Hector is trapped on the overpass between two cops.

HECTOR

Fuck. I'm stuck. This uniform saw me toss that punk onto the third rail. I boogied up the overpass and there was another one waiting for me, like being caught in a rundown after leading too far off first base. Goddamnit. It's too far down to jump, and both of these fuckers have their guns out. I look at the two of them, figure I'll try to jet past the taller one. With a higher center of gravity, it might work, as long as he doesn't shoot me first. I got nothing to lose and everything to gain if I can get the fuck out of here.

CPD OFFICER #1705

This tiny, wide motherfucker comes barreling my way full speed. What am I supposed to do? I already have my weapon out; we had a report of a gang fight in progress with one likely fatality confirmed—dispatch said on-site witnesses were gagging on the smell, so I figured it was legit. I holler freeze but he just keeps coming. My service piece is a .45. I yell again but he isn't quitting. I pop a shot that creases the top of his head, but it doesn't stop him. I hope he's a midget and not some kid as I squeeze off another shot that plows into the back of his neck when he skids into me. Fuck. Writing up a fatality is gonna be almost as shitty as the counseling they'll make me go to.

CPD OFFICER #651

Someone's gonna be on leave for a bit.

TEDDY

Lil Demon and Henry were heading my way. Pepper was passed out on top of me but not dead. Dangit. I could smell the mother-fucker's breath still leaking from his mouth—old bologna, peeled onions, Miracle Whip, and shit whiskey. Plus, I think some of these civilians had pissed their pants. Thought I was gonna puke for sure. I leaned up on an elbow, got a look at his back. Hahaha, shiiiit. He was gonna bleed out. Good. I didn't know what hap-pened, but this peckerwood was fixin' to die, looked like. I thought maybe some karmic hand of justice or something had reached out of the universe but knew deep down that Coyote had looked out for me, just like he had with the cops in the alley, saving my ass yet again. Like he always would for us when we needed him most. I'd put down some tobacco later.

Right now, two chunky cops had Hector trapped on the over-pass. Fuck. I was stuck down here with this greasy redneck crum-pled across my legs bleeding out onto the platform. Shiiiit. Here comes Henry. He can help me get free of this about-to-be corpse. I hollered, "Folks. Get this fucker off me so we can help Hector up there!"

"Shiiiit, bro. He's fucked. We gotta get outta here, Teddy."

"It ain't right, brother. We can't leave him."

"Got no choice, homes."

We heard a shot boom out, then another right after.

Damn it.

"Alright, bro. Help me up." I stuck out my hand.

He hauled me to my feet.

I looked around, then down, kicked Pepper in the face and stomped on his knife hand, booted his Barlow onto the tracks.

Miguel and Walter pulled up, looking kinda sweaty, but fair enough, I saw what they did to those Deuces. Lil Demon was a couple steps behind them.

"What's up, Folks?" I asked.

"You see it, homes." Miguel grinned, that little pull at the corner of his mouth he did, eyes flat and milky gray-white-green, the eyes mixed folks get.

"Right on." I shuddered. "We gotta get out of here, Folks."

"Yuh," Walter agreed, taking off.

"I'm with it," Lil Demon said, doing the same.

Henry said, "Let's fuckin' go," hustled up.

Mikey slapped his chest a couple times, laughed.

We all ran across the platform and over to the stairs. The uniform who'd shot Hector caught my eye. I stopped and stared back at him from the first step, let him know I knew what he did. He might lose some sleep.

Probably not, though.

And then we were downstairs on the landing below the west side of the platform. We watched six or eight more uniforms run up the stairs on the east side. A plainclothes trailing behind them looked our way, made us for gangbangers but we were too far gone. We stumbled down the last flight of stairs and onto the sidewalk.

Shiiit, man. We just fell out laughing. What a fucking day.

"Dang, bro. That shit was crazy," Mikey said.

Miguel shook his head low, laughed. Walter grinned, chewed the inside corner of his mouth. Lil Demon spotted the hot dog place at the station. "Hey, *Demon* Dogs! Gonna have to come back and have one!"

I still heard those two shots, said, "Hector wasn't moving but I could see that big chest still taking shallow breaths. They'll probably take him to Children's or something. We'll need to find out which room, go visit."

"Yeah, yeah, yeah" and "for real" went up along with "fuck those pigs, that was bullshit."

"Speaking of hospitals, you alright, Teddy?" Henry asked.

Guess I was still bleeding. "Yeah, bro, I'm good," I told him. "I got some Krazy Glue. Gonna close that shit right up."

"What the fuck, Krazy Glue?" He laughed a little.

"Yeah, man. I read how they use it instead of stitches sometimes. Good enough for a hospital, good enough for me," I said.

"But if you needed stitches, you probably read about how to do that, too, yeah?" he said.

"For real, bro. I've already done both."

"I ain't surprised, Midget. Not at all." He laughed some more.

"For real, Teddy?" Walter piped up.

"Yeah, homes. Remember when Junior got stabbed on Morse by that Howard Street Lord they call TJ? I got a kit in the Jewel's home section and sewed up that little love handle of his. Prolly coulda glued it, but I didn't know about it then. I put six lime-green stitches in his side. He cut 'em out a couple weeks later, no problem."

"For real, Folks. I remember that," Mikey said.

"Oh yeah. That's right," Henry laughed.

"Damn, Teddy." Miguel shook his head a little more.

Lil Demon leered, shook his head, too.

I thought about it myself. Weird, yeah, but you do what you gotta do, know what you gotta know. I pulled out the glue, popped the top and dripped a couplethree beads onto the cut, squeezed it shut.

"Ain't no thang, Folks," I said. "Just taking care of business."

"Yeah. Always taking care of business, Folks. That's alright," Miguel said.

"I guess so," I said, snapping the cap back into place. We walked on for a bit. I half expected, more hoped, RJ would somehow pop up out of nowhere. He could do shit like that. It would be good to have him here, too, but I knew better. These fumes from the Krazy Glue were a lot. I wondered about those other cats, how they were making out. They'd just sort of disappeared.

Mikey2

Fuck this. I got money. I'm taking a cab. I followed Lil Psycho down the stairs from the platform after Hector fried that guy on the tracks. Ain't no way I'd want to go out like that, holy shit, I could still smell it, probably always would. Yeah, sure, I was up for a good time, maybe fighting some Mexican dudes or whatever, but this shit was nuts. If my old man finds out, I'll be dead for sure, even if I didn't do anything. There's way too much going on back there. What the fuck, people stabbing each other and shit. These guys are serious, way too serious for me. I have to get out of here. I'm taking Lil Capone with me and grabbing the first cab I see. Good thing my dad always makes sure I have money. There was no way I'm getting on the bus. I want to go straight home, hug my ma, pet my dog. Figuring out who was going to live and who was going to die is the last thing I want to do right now. I ain't that guy.

Mikey3

I did *not* sign up for this shit. I think Mikey L. is flagging a cab and I'm getting in on that if he'll let me. These people are crazy. I've got way too many plans for myself to throw it all away on some shit like this. Catching a felony on a weekday afternoon is *not* the way I want to go.

LiL Psycho

In keeping with my "it's an exceptionally good time to get the fuck out of here" program, I decide to slink under the El and through the alleys to make my way over to Belmont hoping they have a delayed Evanston Express sitting at the platform, a train I can take all the way to my dad's place by Northwestern University. This shit got too real too quick. I know I did okay, handled myself, but yeah. A trip to Dad's and some kind of normalcy would really hit the spot. I keep my head down and march on, but a couple blocks down two dudes on crappy house-painted BMX bikes skid up to me, start yelling "Royal Killer!" and shit like that. They look me in my white face, note my long hair and say:

"Oh. He's a headbanger."

"Never mind."

And ride off.

Like I never existed.

Teddy

Me and Mikey walked east on Fullerton. We were gonna catch the Clark Street bus all the way home. After that shit we kinda felt invincible. Fuck it. Henry, Walter, and Miguel had peeled off on their own up the first alley, took Lil Demon and all their Juniors and Peewees with them.

"That shit was wild, right?" I said.

"For real, homes! What the fuck," Mikey said.

"Yeah, dang, bro." We walked by the DePaul Art Museum, right on the avenue, a place I'd never been. I woulda loved to have gone, but I didn't think I could get in. "Needa eat, bro. Not gonna lie."

"Yeah," he agreed.

"Yeah," I said, too, thinking hard about supper.

"Didn't see any of those magic Eagles popping out to help us with all that," he said.

He had a point. "True that," I said. "I ain't all that sure we ever will, with that set."

"You ain't never liked them anyway, ain't it, Folks?"

"Nope," I confirmed. Fuck those assholes.

We got closer to Lincoln Avenue, by the spot they called Aetna Park. A couple of dudes with maroon and aqua big-fin mohawks sailed by on skateboards.

"What's up with this neighborhood anyway, bro?" Mikey asked.

"What do you mean?"

"There's like gangbangers but also these punk rock dudes or whatever." He stuck out his chin at a pile of mohawks cutting hard left to the park.

"Yeah. That's it. It's whatever." I duck-lipped, raised both brows. "I like that."

"Do you miss living down here?"

"Kinda. Sometimes, I guess."

"You're about this artsy music shit, ain't it, Midget?"

"Yeah, I am, bro. But it's alright. If I can't get that, I got books," I said, though I sounded lame as soon as I did.

"That's the truth, bro. I hear you." He rubbed the top of his head, full-teeth smiled at me.

"Still."

"Still what?"

"You know."

"Yeah," he said. "I guess being around it every day is different, ain't it?"

"Yeah. It is. But I'll be alright."

"I know you will."

"You're right about that, Folks," I said.

"We should check on the set, yeah?"

"Yeah, we should."

I turned around to see our folks behind us. We were missing some cats, that's for sure, but all told, we weren't doing too bad. I noticed the other two Mikeys were gone, but I kinda thought that would happen. Looked like Lil Psycho had peeled off, too. I wondered how our man RJ was doing in lockup. Probably about time for those bologna sandwiches. Man, he was gonna be something when he got out tomorrow on an I-Bond. Couldn't wait for him to get back to the neighborhood and complain. That'd be fun.

As we got to the corner of Clark and Fullerton, Mikey spied a pay phone, said, "Wait up a minute, homes. I gotta make a quick call."

"Right on, bro. Do your thing." I went and sat on a much-graffitied bench full of Circle A's and Misfits and Black Flag logos.

The art thing Mikey was talking about is for real and here's how I know: one day I'll have an interview down at the Merc. On a fine spring morning I'll take an A train from the Loyola station down the street from my first apartment at 1249 W. Street with the Same Name as the stop. It's an empty lot now. Probably had to tear the whole building down after they couldn't get my place clean, ha. Holy moly we partied there. A lot.

Anyway, my stepma had arranged a job interview for my

nineteen-year-old self at some fancy trading house instead of the local place I was at. I was already working at the Merc, the Chicago Mercantile Exchange, and had been there or the Board of Trade since a month or two after I got out of the navy. My entry into Uncle Sam's service was my one alternative to spending solid time in Joliet on some narcotics and weapons charges the local GI were *real* horny about pinning on me around a month after I turned seventeen, even if I didn't do it. Three to five downstate or four in the service they said, so anchors aweigh ♪♫ and all that. Sent our boat off to Beirut where I got zero useful civilian training but retired me from gangbanging, I suppose, at least for the moment, which seemed to be what they wanted. Going into the military was kind of the only way out of things, so I enjoyed a sort of retired status when I got home, whether I wanted it or not. And things had changed while I was away, gotten more intense. Everyone was packing and shootings were the only way anything got settled. Humbugs and jumping each other in alleys mostly disappeared, drive-bys were the standard, and dealing had moved up to coke with lots of folks starting to hit the pipe. Prospects were grim, so maybe some kind of regular gig would pay bills. But sitting at home reading *Soldier of Fortune* magazine classifieds and brushing up on Spanish by watching telenovelas on WGBO channel 66 and thinking about heading to Honduras wasn't really job hunting even if it was my only option related to what I did in the navy, so, yeah, after she nagged for a solid few weeks, I wound up in the same business as the old man. And like him, I was inexplicably good at it. Wild, but not surprising, I guess, with our lineage and whatnot.

I started off as a runner working for this Irish guy who was a big drunk. Not trucking in stereotypes just facts, and I'm telling you this because it's the reason I got the job, double time. 1) I was

hanging out with the old man at Yee Wall's during the day, and
Sully came in already buzzed and started pounding beers and big
sweaty Collins glasses of whiskey on the rocks at one-thirty in the
afternoon, and 2) his drunk ass had just fired all fourteen of his
runners after the market closed. Being a runner was an entry-level
gig in the business. You brought the customer's orders from the
phone clerk into the trading pit, back when they had open outcry
and live trading in the pits. You could fuck around and half-ass
the gig if you wanted, never get anywhere, do anything, and still
get paid, or you could apply yourself. The Board was mostly Irish
Catholic traders and pretty low-key compared to the Merc. The
grain floor opened at nine-thirty, closed at one-fifteen. Lots of
folks did coke and even more of them just drank all day. We always
heard that was the best way to trade. It was chaos and high-stakes
risk and sweat and fear and when it was busy, what a rush. It paid
$500 a month to start, but there were lots of side hustles like
slinging dope, errands for traders, favors, gambling, and for me,
playing *Jeopardy!* for dough and drinks against these assholes in the
bar downstairs. At Christmastime cash bonuses and tips in plain
envelopes flew around the floor, and the one time when the lottery got up to a then record $44 million, this big broker group in
the wheat pit gave us a lotto ticket every time we brought out an
order that whole week before the drawing. It was gangstery enough
every now and again to keep me interested for a minute, anyway.

Sitting next to the old man at the very back corner of the bar,
then as now, concerned with sight lines and forever surveilling any
door in and out of the place, I watched this sharp-nosed, Vitalis-
slicked Mick roll toward us, his permanently crooked-at-the-top-
joint forefinger up in the air eternally saying wait a minute next to
his nodding head like a pre-agreement to whatever anyone had to
say, keeping the peace post-violence, and smiling to himself, then

turning those off-white Chiclets our way in a greeting that gulped air and chugged an imaginary drink at the same time.

"Hey, John," the old man said, turning to me, winking.

"Teddy, how the hell are you?" Sully took an adjacent stool.

"Pocałuj mnie w dupę," he said, *kiss my ass* along with "zimne piwo," *cold beer*—the only two things the old man knew how to say in Polish.

Sullivan leered, waved that crookedy finger at Frank the bartender, said, "Old Style with a triple whiskey rocks," and shook his head, no idea what the old man just said, only that it was Polish, and he didn't understand it at all.

"Okay, John," Frank said, pushing his glasses up on his nose and wiping a brown glass hand grenade bottle of Old Style with a bar towel. He opened it, set it down a little hard on a waiting coaster, then turned to fix the highball.

Frank was the only bartender I ever saw at Yee Wall's, the Chinese restaurant with a bar in the back across from the Board of Trade. He was a good guy, liked and disliked the same exact people I did. He was never going anywhere, lived under some kind of penal yoke because he asked out the boss's daughter one time, apparently a big no-no. I'm not sure if it was a class/cultural thing like in Bruce Lee movies or just the owner's rules. Either way, Frank had a defeated and dignified air about him that I couldn't replicate if I had a dozen lifetimes to parlay and forty pages to describe.

The owner was Louie, Uncle Louie to me. He was kind and generous to us, a friend of the family with a magnificent toupee. He was in his mid-eighties at least, so old his eyes had turned that gray-blue-green color; he had a girlfriend, Bea, who was about fifty or so and read palms with disarming accuracy. I'm still living the shit she told me; I check the lines on my hands and say "yup."

Uncle Louie was a player. Him and Bea went to the Bahamas every Christmas. He put this guy Lawson in charge one time, dude who had worked there for years, but Lawson ran gambling and girls out of the restaurant while Uncle Louie was working on Bea and his tan, asked me if I wanted in on either. Come January, Lawson disappeared. Uncle Louie just smirked and waved his hands when someone at the bar asked about him. When my stepma passed, he sent a six-foot wreath of white lilies to the funeral, so yeah, he was the real deal. Uncle Louie also gave the old man a plain white envelope once or twice a month; he'd stuff it in an inside coat pocket, and I wouldn't see it again. I never found out why, or what it was, and I never asked. There're some things you don't need to know about.

I started drinking in Uncle Louie's restaurant when I was about thirteen, one Saturday night after the last time the old man took me school-clothes shopping at Montgomery Ward's. I bought baggies and flannels, just like I did the other day. I've been in and out of style three times now. When I started out my twenty-first birthday in the afternoon at Yee Wall's, Uncle Louie slow made his way to the back corner of the bar, put his arm around me and said:

"Hey, Speedy. How old are you now, thirty?" He laughed until he coughed, and bought me a beer. Speedy was my old man's nickname for me. I didn't start walking until I was three or so, about the time I started reading. Apparently, I scooched on my ass everywhere I went, and I was fast. No one except the old man and my aunts and uncles ever called me by my nickname, no exceptions. One guy tried, one of my Irish bosses from the suburbs who eventually had to make up his own nickname for me because I'd never answer him otherwise. He made Frank's *and* the old man's don't-like list. Dude is on my own list to this day, 'cause I hold a grudge like that; sometimes it's forgive, maybe, but it's always never forget. He tried to message me on social media a year or so ago. I left him on read for three months and then said, "Oh hey. What's up." Never heard back. Fuck that guy.

"Teddy, I had to fire all my runners today. Jesus Fucking Christ, I've never seen a more fucked-up group." John sighed, lit a Marlboro 100, ran his hand over all that slicked-back black hair. He was a floor manager at the Board for a good-sized local discount house. That meant lots of little and a few medium whiny accounts along with one big fat one to pay most of the bills and take up everyone's attention.

"Jesus, John." The old man shook his head, took a drink of his vodka and Coke. "What are you gonna do now?"

"Fuck. I'll have to find people. And get the phone clerks to fill in." He drained off half his whiskey.

"That ain't gonna work, John. Phone clerks are lazy shits." The old man laughed.

"Who's this?" the Irishman asked, looking over at me.

"That's Speedy. My oldest," he said, lit a cigarette.

"Great. What's he do?" Sully asked.

"Ask him yourself," the old man said, snapping his Zippo shut.

"Well? What do you do, then?" Sully asked, the rude fuck.

"Usually what I want, but lately what I do is look for jobs."

"Any luck?"

"I'm here at two in the afternoon. What do you think?"

"Touché."

"Got that right."

"Sorry, kid. All good?" He softened a little.

"Yeah. All good. Hey, listen. I *could* use a job. You got anything for me after you let go of all those folks working for you? There must be something."

"Can you hear thunder and see lightning?"

"Yeah."

"You're hired. See you down here at nine in the morning."

It all went well, I learned a pile of shit, including how to get up early. Like I said, I'm kind of a night person, so this was an adjustment. Anyway, after a month or so, yay technology creep, we got CRTs, computer relay terminals, down on the trading floor as a way to send confirmations on filled orders back to our bigger customers, normally the job of phone clerks, but we already know about their work ethic, right?

I BS'd my way into the CRT job by telling John I had used a computer when I was in the navy. I figured, how hard could it be? I usually have a pretty short learning curve, and this was no exception. Once I had that down, the boss asked if I wanted to learn how to check trades. The trade-checking gig is just making sure that for every buy there's a sell and for every sell there's a buy and that the commodity, price, and month all match up. The job interview this whole part is supposed to be about was for a new gig doing the trade-checking thing. It was real good money for a high school dropout with a GED. I actually ended up going just about as far as I could as a non-trader with no college could: operations manager. But everything is gone now; the pits are in museums and all the trading is done electronically except for maybe Eurodollars and butter or something. No big loss for customers, though. There was a whole lot of shady shit going down, especially in the currencies. I'm happy to tell you about "guaranteed fills in the opening range" anytime you want to know. Fuck. If I ever remember it all I'll be happy to tell the Commodity Futures Trading Commission, too, for that matter, for some money, anyway. Those dudes took white-collar crime to a-whole-nother level, some real sheisty rich-boy shit for sure, and yup, I checked. Lots of them went down for all kinds of violations a few years after I left the biz. Even though I don't like to use the word, it would seem that karma is, indeed, a bitch.

But a couple years after I started, like I said, I'd learned enough that I could go look for better jobs in the business and that was where I was headed today, courtesy of my stepma. And I guess it was a good day to reflect on how I'd got to this place in life so all that what-what was running through my brain as I walked up Monroe from the State Street stop to the Merc. Holy moly. I got to the interview early. I'm pathologically tardy to everything, so this was already odd and made me think of the very first day I started working at the Board of Trade. I was the new guy, so I got the 10:30 a.m. lunch slot. Twenty minutes to eat. Oh boy. It was a weird not-time downtown, anyway, not a whole lot going on, streets awful quiet. I went to the dumpy Burger King on Monroe just west of La Salle. Worst time of the day—is it breakfast? Is it lunch? You get what you get, and either way, it's quick. The Board is at Jackson and La Salle, so it was a straight shot over a couple streets to Monroe. I crossed against the light to the north side of the street, and turned up the block, already halfway through a cigarette. I knocked the cherry off, blew out the stale smoke to save the half for later, stuck it back in the pack, and looked up to see this long-haired dude in a black leather biker jacket just bopping down the sidewalk toward me. I'm thinking where've I seen this guy before? Holy shit, it was Alice Fucking Cooper. As we were about to pass each other, it just came out and I said right there in my man's face:

"Holy shit. It's Alice Fucking Cooper." I whipped around watching him go.

"Fuckin A, dude," he said, walking backward, giving me the double devil horns.

They had some croissan'wiches left, so I got one with ham, and a coffee.

Later on, after asking around, I found out Alice Fucking Cooper lived at Lake Point Towers, in case that sounds like bullshit to you. Maybe he was out taking a nice long walk, or went to look at the river instead of just that beautiful view of Lake Michigan, who knows? But he sure seemed happy, and that was cool, aspirational. Me though, right now, not so much. I sat full on the edge of one of those industrial-sized planters that can grow whole-ass trees in them, along with seasonal flowers they always wait just a little too long to change out, so they curl and die, and add to the depression brought on by seeing neglected ideas of urban beautification. Sometimes the city is thoughtlessly cruel—maybe sometimes by design, but always by laziness.

I slow bumped the heels on my black suede Hush Puppies against the planter, smoked a cigarette, and killed time I'd never get back, a fact I increasingly resented as the sun tilted higher over the lake, this sunny mid-spring day, one of those few magic ones we get in Chicago, usually in the first week of May before it turns to 90 degrees with 100 percent humidity until early September. I had on a white dress shirt (don't laugh) along with a black leather skinny tie and a pair of pine-colored baggies. Sweaty clerks and sweatier traders zipped back and forth, hurrying to places that mattered only to them. Women in skirts and white running shoes hustled head down with briefcases and purses I was supposed to know the name of, Aqua Net auras and perms crackling in the sun that lifts all the light in town when the clouds clear off. I thought about the original Board of Trade site, a place on the Chicago River where ancestors of mine would visit for tens of thousands of years, a convenient and logical place appropriated by settlers like most big cities in this country, places where Native folks had met and traded objects of need and desire, along with intellectual concerns and spiritual matters and philosophies, and language and kinship, alliances and strife, loves and wars, all humanity has to offer, since time immemorial.

And while I was sitting there thinking about all this shit, she walked by. A magenta mohawk with lime-green bangs hanging down on one side, black leggings that ended in worn black ten-hole Docs, red Dress Stewart flannel tied around her waist, a black lace bustier and jean shorts under her black leather Chicago cop jacket, hefting a big fat portfolio filled with what I was sure were the world's most exciting sketches, paintings, and onion skin ideas for even greater work. Was that my wife someday? Maybe. Probably. I think I'm married to her right now. I'll have to ask her about that day in *her* life sometime. But for sure, she lived in a world right then I wanted to be in one day.

And what was I doing that morning? Something that would never even let me visit it.

So, I did it. Said fuck it. Flicked my cigarette onto Wacker Drive, dusted off my ass, and headed back to State Street to catch the El home. Thought, then laughed, about stopping at that Burger King on Monroe, went with saving my money for a gyro from Papa Dees on Sheridan by the house. I had one of those absolutely-in-the-moment moments, the ones where you know you're making a decision that'll change your whole life, one of those short windows where you're in tune with the universe, a fully aware glimpse at the big, big picture you might get two or three, even four times in your life if you're lucky and learn how to pay attention, how to look for them. The recommitment to make art, to live for art, is the reason I'm writing this to you right now. If we don't have art, what do we have? What's the point? To make money for some asshole? Nah. There's gotta be more or it just ain't worth it.

Hey now. Here comes Miguel, Walter, Henry, Lil Demon, some Juniors, and a pile of Peewees out of the alleyway right before Clark Street. Who knows what they been doing? Let's find out.

MiGUEL

"Yo, Teddy, can you hook us up with an AR from those Christiana and Wellington boys? I know you know them cats." He's sitting plain as day, but it's like he's anywhere but here. I look at him, really stare at him for a full minute, anyway, no talking. He gets this weird smile on his face and says, "Yeah. I think so. Just one?" No laughing.

Pffft. Well damn, I think. This motherfucker. We can get more than one?

"If you could get a pair, that'd be cool, Folks." What else are you gonna say?

"Cool, cool, Folks. I'll see what I can do," he says.

I wasn't too sure about that, say, "Aight, Folks. Appreciate it."

Maybe shoulda called him Lil Fixer instead of Midget.

"Ain't nothing, Folks," he says. "I got you. But what we really need to talk about is how much they got their thing on lock. Shiiiit. They got cops on their side."

Teddy has some ideas about government, what the neighborhood means. Talks about community and whatnot, acts like we're a for real tribe or some. Whatever he needs to do, I guess, as long as he takes care of business.

"Cool, Folks," I say. "Let's set something up."

He winks like an old guy and goes back to talking shit with Mikey, who had just hung up the pay phone.

Mikey

Can't believe Miguel asked for two ARs. Farwell was gonna be lit this summer if Teddy comes through with that shit, even one of those. The meeting looked like all kinda chaos, but I saw Teddy talking to those C/W dudes, some of those other Albany Park whiteboys and then some of those BGDs from the West Side. Dude had connections. And if he didn't, he would make them. I think it was about to get really real back home. The meeting mighta seemed like a bust, but it was a game changer, I have a feeling. Shit was gonna change, and quick. We saw it today with those fool GLs just doing a casual drive-by on a few hundred Folks. Seemed like we were moving into a serious new era of really real. Not sure I was ready for alla that, but it was coming, whether I liked it or not.

Teddy

After Miguel and them took off to who knows where this time, we hopped on the Clark Street bus. Made the rest of our way over to the stop, zero conflict. We got on, no problems; the driver took our transfers, didn't even look at them. He was an old black dude, older than we'd ever get to be, and he seemed supremely tired by that fact. I didn't think too much about it then, but I did plenty when I was older. Ever notice how there's not too many older dudes of color? My own brown dad would pass at sixty-two, and even at my age now I think that's not so bad. This world just kills us off and no one says shit. You ever see really old-ass brown and Black dudes? Not really. Me neither.

Even though it was less crowded after a bunch of yuppies got off at Fullerton, it was still pure shit. We sat confined with windows that wouldn't open and an air-conditioning unit that might've worked five years ago. It was stuffy and packed with Big Ten state school assholes who were gentrifying the neighborhoods farther north. They looked sweaty as fuck in their cheapish suits and power blouses with running shoes, uncomfortable in their own pale skins, lives of lame office hookups and hopes for big suburban houses already carved deep in their sad, doughy faces, quick flips on North Side condos with dreams of fat down payments on Barrington starter homes already out of their fat-handed Iowa and Wisconsin clutches. There were people I hated in the world, but none like these pieces of shit. It would be easy to feel sorry for them, but that's not how my universe worked. The quicker they got mugged and moved away, the better.

The bus moved too slow, the humidity and Aramis/Polo making me gag. A couple of older cats who looked like PR Stones, or maybe even old-school PBCs, Paulina Barry Community dudes, got on and instantly wilted in the money and heat, too tired to talk shit to us in the back of the bus. Their wispy mustaches seemed even more disappointed than we were. For real. We gotta get off this thing. I leaned back, watched a Clark Street that used to be roll by.

I'm sure I wasn't the only one who picked up on the vibe that rolled out over us that day. This was going to be something new to lots of us, new for the city, too. There were gonna be plenty of opportunities to make things bigger and better for ourselves, and I had to always keep us at the front, family first. I thought all the time about what Coyote said, about taking care of them, helping the community, but I also had to think about what this would mean in the long run, too. There were more and more developers with state school university grads filling their cheap shitboxes made out of our old places and hangouts all the time. Old Man Daley was gone, and we had our first woman mayor, Jane Byrne. She'd even gone to St. Scholastica's in our neighborhood right there on Ridge Blvd. Things were opening even as others were shutting down. A new decade was just around the corner and fears were as high as expectations. Progress can be great and cruel all in the same moment.

Mikey

"How do you do that?" I ask, leaned back, glaring at the ceiling in this hot, shitty bus.

"Do what?" Teddy asks, staring out the window.

"Just be knowing folks, or talking to them like you do?" I look his way.

"What do you mean, Folks?" He turns to face me.

"You know, like with them cats from the other branches up at the meeting. I saw you with those C/W dudes, or A/S or whatever they were, talking with them whiteboys about rifles and shit. Shit like that." I watch my own face talking in his sunglasses.

"I 'on't know. You just do," he says. He rubs at his greasy nose with both hands. The shine disappears for a second or two, comes right back.

"Maybe *you* just do, but *we* don't," I say.

"It's just a thing, I guess. If you know what you want, nothing else matters. You tell yourself that and the words just come out. I can't really explain it. It's like someone else is talking when it happens. Then later you have to remember what you said."

"Shiiiit. That's wild. Ain't it creepy?"

"Nah. Well, okay, maybe the first couple of times, but then you know when it starts happening, and you let it."

"Don't think I could do it, homes," I say.

"You could if you didn't have a choice, bro." He smiles big but kinda sad.

"Damn."

"Yeah. Damn," he says.

TEDDY

When we crossed under the El tracks at Roscoe, I looked straight out this big bus window at Clark Street, then up above to see trains running in both directions. Damn, the CTA was efficient sometimes. You'd think a dead kid on the third rail would hold things up, but I guess since it wasn't a whiteboy they just moved on. Anyway, fuck this.

Me and Mikey got off the bus at Addison, walked down toward the train station. The rest of the set can ride the bus all the way north, but we're taking the El home. Fuck the bus. I still felt a little lucky and had some tokens left over. When we hit the platform, we saw they made the train an all-stops to Wilson because of the shit at Fullerton, so for the first time in our lives we grabbed an A train at Addison. Surreal. And kick-ass, 'cause we were going to Jarvis, which was an A-stop, and we wouldn't have to get off at Wilson to switch for one. Sometimes life was okay.

It was kind of a long ride north from here, but it would be good to chill for a bit. The train wasn't too crowded, plenty of folks I guessed had been rerouted or shied away from the commotion farther south. Me and Mikey sat in the first two-seater off the doors on the right-hand side of the car. He was slouched down, leaned back on the headrest, hands and fingers twined over his chest, looking deep in thought.

"What you thinking about, man?" I asked, thought he must be tired. It was a pretty big day after all.

"Nothing, man. Nothing at all," he said, ran his hand over his head slow.

We rocked in silence for a while, late-day hot steel wheels complaining against the rails every now and again. The sun was quick dipping low on the prairies to the west, sending out wild beams to find us between darkening buildings as we rolled along.

I leaned forward in my seat, the heat of one shooting through the window to rest on my face.

"What should I do about that?" I said, closing an eye against the light.

Mikey stared at me for ten or fifteen seconds, said, "Don't do that, bro. Remember?"

"Right. What should I do about those ARs Miguel asked for?" I pulled out my lighter, flicked it.

"Do what Miguel wants, I suppose," Mikey said. "You should probably get us a couple, too."

"For real?" I stared at the flame.

"Yeah. Why not?"

"I don't know, man. Guns don't sit quiet. Folks are gonna shoot or find a reason to. Makes me kinda nervous. Guns get guns, know what I'm saying?"

"Yeah, I do. But guns are coming anyway. Might as well be strapped, too, Midget." Mikey rubbed his head.

"Wanna go between the cars and have a smoke?" I asked.

"Nah, man. I'm good. But go ahead if you want."

"Nah. It's cool. I can wait," I said.

Magic light, golden hour, is an amazing time anywhere, but in Chicago it's otherworldly. Maybe it happens only if you're from here, in a for-real way, but every alley, back porch, park, boulevard, lake, lagoon or river, skyscraper, zoo, school, bridge, or train track shows off its ghosts, their spirits shimmering beside, behind, and above them, frail and pale blue gray, silver highlights cut fleeting outlines at the edge of your vision, all of it coming together to impart an unnamable feeling of calm and wonder that'll make you get up the next morning just to wait all day for it to come again. If you know where and how to look, you can see pheasants and foxes, coyotes and eagles, badgers and bobcats all doing their thing.

So many of my ancestors are here some days the golden hour feels like a rowdy family reunion. Even my mother's side of the family goes back a couple of generations. The old man's goes back a thousand. I have ancestors and relatives from all Three Fires Confederacy and a couple more nations who visited and traded here. Chicago lives in and on my body in ways I'll never be able to explain, no matter how many words I learn, how many dictionaries and encyclopedias I read. And I'm good with that. To belong to a place that belongs to you, that claims you eternally and always has, what more could you ask for?

I rested my head on the big dirty window, eye up close to a V/L and five-pointed star etched into the glass, looked through it and watched my great-grandparents' mom and dad slow dance on the third floor back porch of a shitheap building on Wilton Avenue. The Sheridan stop was two minutes away. I pulled out the glue and set it between my legs on the seat. I checked the blood on my arm. It had slowed to a trickle but was still coming through the gummy scab trying to form in the wound. I wiped it all out with the bottom of my T-shirt. I popped the top off the Krazy Glue, held the bottom in my teeth and let it drip into the cut while I squeezed the edges together. When it was full, I spit the top out onto the seat next to me and waited for the glue to dry, blowing on it, watching the blood mix with the clear sealant.

Coyote fuzzed in a few rows up.

Whatcha doing, nephew, he asked, lighting a cigarette in the middle of the car.

Great, I thought. The conductor comes through here and I'm gonna get blamed for smoking, probably get kicked off. I looked over at Mikey, but apparently it was his turn to pass right out. No snoring, though, so that was nice.

"Nothing, Coyote," I said, low. "Just heading home."

That's it? he asked.

"Yeah. That's all I got, Old Man. Something else you wanna hear?"

Maybe a thanks, yeah? I saved your ass back there.

"Isn't that your job?" I said.

No. I do what I want.

"But if I'm praying to your raggedy ass, aren't you obligated to help me?"

Not if I don't want to, he said.

"Oh, I think you are, Uncle. Like it or not."

You didn't hand me no obagi. Know what that is? So you're wrong about that one, youngblood. He grinned.

"I don't think I am, Old Man. Ain't my fault no one taught me. But you can tell yourself whatever you want. Ain't no one judging."

Creator is keeping score. But don't worry yourself about that, yeah?

I *was* a little worried but couldn't show it. "I ain't, Coyote. Just make sure you answer prayers."

Oh, I do, young stuff. Like always, keep an eye out for the people, but don't forget to keep one on your own self, yeah? And learn the protocols.

"Always, Old Man. Don't worry about me."

I won't. Unless you ask me to. Properly, from now on. Obagi, boy. And on that note, can you leave me alone for a bit?

"Whatever, man. Don't worry about it."

Fine, then. I won't.

"Don't."

Coyote winked out, way crisper than he had fuzzed in, his disappearance an audible pop in the train car. Since no one had noticed his arrival, his departure was even less of an event this time around. Except to me. I thought about what he had said, the way he left me on my own, no teachings. It was typical, but not terrible. I was used it.

And now I'd have to ask around about this obagi business.

That was the thing about Coyote. He taught some things, but made you look for the rest of the answers. Stuff would come out of his mouth that seemed like rules or whatnot, and you needed to know those protocols, sure, but that was *never* the point; you were supposed to think deeper about it all. At the end you knew way more than when you started, and I suppose that was the point, whether he knew it or not. I suspected he did, but that way he moved through the world never let you know, and I supposed that was also the point. Damn it. Yeah. Coyote was the shit. For real.

Sheridan was an A-stop. We pulled in and out quick. A couple of state school fuckwads hauled their dumpy Iowa asses onto the platform, leaving some of their less fortunate brothers on the train to journey north to even crappier accommodations while they headed down to their sad apartments, TV dinners, and shitty sitcoms on tonight's menu. Maybe some laundry and a regretful call home to Mom in Dubuque.

Suffer.

Now we were on the long haul to Wilson. We passed St. Mary of the Lake, where years ago I was baptized most surely against my tiny half-breed will. On our left in a minute the dying sun would run over the tops of headstones and mausoleums in Graceland Cemetery while on our right it bounced off the back porches and red bricks of dying buildings along Kenmore, Sunnyside, and Broadway in the neighborhood where I was born and raised for a while: Uptown. I always caught tons of feelings riding through here. The place where you came into the world will do that to you, I guess. The way the light was showing off today, like maybe it was gonna be the last day of summer ever, wasn't making it easy to ignore them. The all-stops station was just ahead. Tons of rails and switches and sheds announced that this used to be a big-time yard, a place of importance. I could probably look it up and find out that it used to be an interchange with some other rail lines and was a hub that mattered, but I'd rather let its ghosts sleep along like they deserved.

Like I said, this was mostly Royal territory, but there were still some hillbilly Gaylords that showed up every now and again, along with the occasional pair of Kings, the way they always seemed to travel. I sat up as we pulled into the station, looked around, didn't see anything worth caring about and went back to looking out the window. The PA crackled, the conductor mumbled some shit I couldn't understand except for "next stop, Argyle," and off we went. Mikey snored a little as the train jerked into motion.

I let him sleep, stepped into the warm wind and roar between the doors, lit a cigarette, kept an eye on him through the glass. Not too many folks in the car. I slow smoked while he slept. No sound came to me except the screech of rails and the rush of air all around, its pressure on my eardrums changing as we blew past the Lawrence Avenue B-stop. Mikey looked peaceful, like maybe nothing sounded off inside his head right now, and he was catching a break where he could, something I'd like to have myself. Maybe later, I thought.

Maybe.

Right now, though, I couldn't update those thoughts because there were still a couple of sweaty, witless victims of capitalism on this

A train who were giving the two of us dirty looks right here in our own city. I checked clear paths to the exits, wished I was packing. Nothing should or could pop off on a train car with these big corn-feds, but you never knew. I'd seen enough wild shit go down on the El to never, ever feel completely comfortable.

Mikey snored a little, moved his head. I seized on the moment.

"Bro, are you awake?" I said.

"Nah, man. I'm still asleep."

"No. Get up," I said, looking at the restless Opies on the train. "We gotta be awake, homes. I don't trust these ginger motherfuckers."

"You worry too much, bro."

"Not with these white folks, homes. They're unpredictable, Folks."

"I'll let you worry, then. I'm okay, man."

"Fine. Be that way. I'll take it on for both of us."

"Whatever you gotta do, bro."

"Yup. Whatever."

Turned out I didn't have to do nothing, and all Mikey had to do was fall back asleep. They really were just mad at the world in general; sweaty and pissed at their station in life, Big Ten business degrees right up there with two years' experience working at McDonald's when they got to the city. These cats were probably runners at the commodity exchanges, entry-level pukes working on the trading floor and wasting working folks' time in back offices downtown. I knew them well because I'd have to train and supervise them three and four at a time someday. Every now and then there'd be one I'd have to be nice to because his uncle was a big account at the house. But right now, I just had to be glad their rage didn't boil over into a blip on the five o'clock news.

The big fat sun blazed red, red, red through the greasy glass windows, angling over one of Chicago's biggest cemeteries. Whenever

I had the urge, which was more than occasionally, much to my detriment, I'd grab a 40 and then head in to spit on Kinzie's and Pinkerton's graves; a lying sack of shit and an anti-union asshole always deserved that disrespect. But for real, there were decent folks there like Jack Johnson and Ernie Banks, so it wasn't a total loss, and as a necropolis, it was amazing, like St. Louis in New Orleans, a boneyard I'd visit one day, just to try and find Marie Laveau's spot. Yeah, for sure these motherfuckers weren't worth the time of day, but still, I thought about that shit. Knowing history can be a blessing but thinking about it all the time can be a curse. I embraced both, though, figured it was part of the deal, was glad to take it on. Elders always said we're only our stories, it's important to keep them alive, and what were our stories but the best kinds of history kept and shared?

It wasn't easy to preserve all these stories, keep them fed and quiet until the right time came for them to roll out. There was maintenance involved, addition and evolution.

Stories are living things, told and exercised, reviewed by the People for accuracy, for humor and usefulness. Accuracy and insight, timeliness and necessity. All those things evolve over time.

Truth lives in moments of need and stories are the lifeblood of a community. It's essential that they're scrutinized and approved. Getting them wrong can be deadly, especially for the teller.

Watching the keepers of stories is essential to the would-be weaver. Timing and timeliness, rhythm, volume, inflection, delivery. Those skills took years to learn, let alone master. Was there a harder job? Probably not. Was there a better one?

No.

Definitely not.

This Marlboro was only half-done, but I wasn't gonna waste it, so I stayed between the doors as we stopped at Argyle, kept an eye on Mikey still passed out through the window. No one even got on the car, and we were rolling again in seconds. The next stop wasn't until Bryn Mawr, though, so I'd be able to finish my smoke no problem. The long day scrolled by in my mind, and I picked at its problem moments, tried to learn from them.

A couple things started to come into focus on their own, but then I decided to take the lead for myself, pushed into the future, did that thing. Yeah. Not good.

It would be hot, and slower than Death on stilts, Chicago slouching through the last days of August and Mikey thinking he's broke as shit, needing to make some dough before fall hit and the rhythm of the neighborhood would tilt toward school and work, summer street hustles cooling close to stillness.

A simple burn would do the trick. A guy who'd been asking around to buy some weed in bulk made the perfect mark. Give him a good price on a couplethree pounds and a shopping bag full of newspapers with some nice buds bricked in plastic wrap across the top at the drop and be on his way. He'd get a couple of the fellas to go with him and make an easy score.

It would all go well until they were walking off with the cash and the mark decided to run his hands across *all* of his new stash. As soon as he hit the newspaper he dropped the bag and grabbed his piece, squeezed off a few on his .25. Mikey'd get one in a hot spot, no chance to fire back, DOA on the sidewalk.

But that would be then and this would be now. Not today, Satan. Not for *tona* years.

Flying past the Berwyn station, I smoked and watched the passengers in the cars on either side of us, folks on their way home from work, looking tired and distracted. Their faces said a lot, said it all, really. Your face is your ad to the world, the cover of your book, but you get to change it whenever you want, as long as you remember you can, and it looked like these folks had forgotten that, or given up on it. I've tried out all kinds of faces with the adults who drift in and out of my life, but they don't actually see them, or maybe worse, they do, and don't care. It's alright, I guess, because the only time my real face shows is with folks like the clown I'm watching sleep right here, and Mikey and the rest of my crew can mock it all they want, 'cause they know I'll do the same to theirs.

I turned around and finished my square as we were pulling into the Bryn Mawr all-stops station, could see people sitting on the benches when I looked through the windows in the car to my right. I timed it perfectly and flicked my cigarette through the gap so it smacked the front page of this business guy's *Tribune,* the cherry exploding on Daley's face, still front-page news even though he passed three or four years ago, hot red sparks and ash flying everywhere as he jumped up from his seat, all mad and scared at the same time. I laughed and went inside to wake up Mikey.

Still shaking off visions of the future, I snuck up close to his ear.

"Pow! Pow! Wake up, Folks!"

"Man, fuck you!" Mikey's head reared back, eyes rolling. Shit. This motherfucker had been *out.* Whoops.

"Calm down, bro. It's all good," I said, patting him on the shoulder.

"What the fuck, Teddy."

"Sorry, man."

"That ain't cool, homes," he said, rubbed his head.

"Duuude. Relax. You're alright, Mikey," I said, way happier with the outcome in the present.

"Dang. Dang, Folks. What the fuck." He blew out a big breath.

I laughed. "Man. You were tired for real."

"For real, homes," he agreed. "Where we at?" His eyes searched the windows.

"Close to home. On our way to Thorndale now. Only four stops to go."

"Alright." He relaxed a little, said, "Bet. You were right, you know."

"About what?" I said.

"About that whiteboy segregation shit." He chewed the inside corner of his lip.

"What do you mean," I said.

"Bro, Pepper tried to stab you. What the fuck." He slapped his chest once, knitted his brows, tilted his head, and gave me the look.

"Tried? Shiiiit. He did," I said.

"Yeah, but not that bad."

"Guess not," I agreed. "Coulda been worse."

"For real," Mikey said. "You wanna talk about why it wasn't?"

"Probably not right now," I said, thinking about Coyote. "Maybe later, okay, homes?"

"Sure, Folks," he said. "No problem."

I didn't want to think too much more about it right now, wanted to talk about it even less. Shit. I kind of don't want to tell *you* about it, even if I should. I guess we could say that Coyote was there because he needed to be, even if it wasn't for me, it was for the stories. All we are are our stories. Sure, stories are truths we tell to keep ourselves sane, but they're also lies we tell to keep others from losing it, too. And it's how we're still going, how our folks are alive in the world. My grandpa said, and elders have always told me, you *have* to tell our stories, they're what keep us as a people alive. So maybe that's it, yeah? I'm supposed to tell them, and Coyote could see I was about to not be doing that in this world much longer. Coyote would know—he knows it all before it happens and how it went down after it did, how it would go next time, the time after that, every other time it would happen.

And if Coyote is dedicated to anything, it's the stories.

Yeah then, as usual, I was lucky. It happens a lot. But so long as I know it, respect it, recognize it, I think it will keep coming my way. I try to appreciate it, though I don't have a system in place to do that, to acknowledge it, understand it, just pray and give thanks to Creator, to Tunkasila, to Gichi-Manidoo. I don't know anyone else who has this happen to them on the regular, or if there's even anybody else out there like this. Maybe someday I'll meet someone who can help me process this in the right ways, respect it like I should, but until then I'll build my own structure around it in the ways I know how, make my vows and promises to Creator and keep them the best I can.

Fuuuck. That's enough of that.

We were through the Loyola station, almost to Morse, where we'd started this long-ass day.

"Homes. You coming over for supper or what?" I asked.

"You mean eat a bunch of tortillas? Meeting Juanita, bro. I told you that," Mikey said.

Shit. He was serious. "Folks. You're delusional *and* dedicated. I admire that in you," I laughed.

"Man, fuck you, Teddy."

"Come on, bro. For real."

"I'm serious, man."

"Alright, Folks. Have it your way," I said. "Wait. Is that who you were calling on the phone?"

He leaned both arms over the seat in front of him, looked out the window at the almost dark.

I recognized my cues, slumped deep in my own seat, pulled out *Boss,* read the cover copy, praise, and intros for the hundredth time, put it away, wondered what was at the house for food.

We snaked down the line, a little slower now, maybe since we were closer to the end of the run at Howard, post–rush hour train yard traffic backing things up a bit. No worries here; I ain't in no hurry for once.

Morse Avenue station came and went without incident, Mikey staring out the window, me up at the ceiling. It would be good to finally get off the train, I supposed.

The intercom crackled, our bored conductor said, "Jarvis. Next stop, Jarvis."

Holy shit. This was it. What a day.

"You ready, homes?" I asked Mikey.

"For sure, Folks. Let's get it," he said.

The train jerked to a stop, and we got off at what I guess was our home stop, almost every inch of the platform covered with our tags, our names, our sets. It was just about dark; long shadows from the tall, golding maples lining Jarvis Avenue angled sharp down the street, ran east to the lake where they disappeared into the inky blue-black over the big water, the final, most magic moments of light dying in spectacular fashion.

"TOLD YOU, FOLKS!" Mikey hollered.

My shoulder burst into flames. Fuck.

"What, Folks?!" I flinched.

"She's here, bro. Juanita is here."

I'll be damned. She was on the sidewalk below, just east of the viaduct on the north side of the street, leaning against the wall. But something was wrong. Mikey hadn't seen it yet, probably because he was so excited just to see her. She was hurt, head down, left arm holding her right high up near the shoulder. Her long black hair covered her face.

"Folks, slow down," I said. "I think something's up. Is she okay?"

"What do you mean?" he said.

"I think she's hurt, bro."

Mikey took off running. I hustled behind him.

We flew down the stairs, burst through the heavy old wooden doors and onto the street.

"Hey, girl," Mikey said, loud, marching across the street, not bothering to look. "Hey. You okay?"

She shook her head so slightly you'd miss it blinking. Mikey must've been, or he was trying to keep things positive.

"Alright, Juanita." He beamed. "I knew you'd make it," he said. "I told this fool." He jerked his thumb at me standing off to the side, directly under the tracks. A southbound B train roared through the station overhead.

Her face tilted up and I saw a big purple shiner where her clear brown left eye should be, puffy and closed. Damn. Her right one caught mine and I just bowed my head, shook it slow. Ouch. But I didn't ask, let Mikey do that.

"What happened?"

She wasn't crying, gave no indication she was in any kind of pain at all.

"A couple of Queens" was all she said.

"Damn. When?" Mikey asked.

"About fifteen minutes before your train pulled in," she said.

You know I was pissed. We'd been to this big meeting, heard all about this new Nation, how we were gonna roll on the streets, look out for Folks, and this bullshit had happened right in our own hood. Wasn't nobody looking out for us up here. We were on our own, and probably always would be.

"Shiiiit. Where the fuck they at now?" he said.

"They took off, fool," Juanita said. "I told them a bunch of Royals were on their way back here from a big meeting. They didn't wanna stick around for that."

"Damn straight," Mikey said. "What the fuck. Who were they?"

"I didn't know the one chick," Juanita said. "Some Korean-looking girl. But the other one was that fuckin' redheaded white chick. Man, I hate that bitch."

"Fuck. Me too," Mikey said.

Yeah. Me too. I knew who she was talking about. Cornrow ginger. Just mean.

"Who gave you the shiner?"

"She did. The white girl."

"Damn."

"Mmmm-hmmm," she agreed. "Damn. But whatever. I'll get her back."

Mikey laughed a little. "I know you will."

I grinned at her. She winked, let it open slow.

"So where are you kids off to?" I asked with a half smirk and raised eyebrow.

"Fuck you, Dad," Mikey said.

It was my turn to laugh a bit, too.

"Whateeever, Gramps," Juanita said, with a snort of her own.

"Damn." I shook my head. "That's just cold."

She winked. "You deserve it, old man."

Mikey put his arm around her, and she leaned in close.

"Alright, you two," I mock-sighed, in full fake-Dad eye roll, "let's get the fuck outta here."

"Fine, den, homes," Mikey said. "S'go."

"S'go." Juanita smirked.

We walked west on Jarvis, those two in their own world, me in mine. By the time we got to Clark Street, it was dark. We crossed over, walked up Rogers, under the Northwestern tracks.

"Be good, kids." I winked, heading south before we crossed Honore.

"We will, Dad," they said together, holding hands.

I walked backward for ten or twenty steps, happy for them. They waved and wove across Pottawattomie Park toward Mikey's place on Birchwood. I lit a cigarette, walked over to the loading dock at Jackass Leather on the corner, sat on the edge of the heavy rubber padding and watched them make their way. Moths dive-bombed the safety lights at the corners of the dock. I listened to their wings softly click on the amber glass and finished my smoke, then hopped down and headed for home. I could just make out a B train zipping through the Jarvis stop, then pulling up quick in the yard at Howard Street, its brakes sounding like they might not make it. That possibility was what I entertained myself with on my way home.

It was pure dark when I dragged my ass into the crib, night coming quicker by the day late in the summer. I flicked the lights on. It smelled like cigarettes and stale beer. The sunporch windows were wide open, and an A train was pulling into Jarvis station. I closed all three crosshatched panes, the noise and haze from the street more than I wanted right now. I made my way to the bathroom, grabbed the peroxide from under the sink, poured a bunch on the cut, found a big gauze pad in the medicine cabinet along with that white cloth tape, bandaged up my arm.

The little light was on over the stove, just the way I liked it, the way I still like it. I pulled the pack of tortillas out of the fridge along with some salsa and a tub of sour cream, turned on the front right burner and made a little supper. I ate off a paper towel 'cause I hate doing dishes and well that's a built-in napkin, so it all works out.

While I was wolfing down those tortillas, Mikey called me. He asked if I found out Hector's room yet, talked again about how Pepper got stabbed at the humbug. He told me folks were saying

Sir Knight did the deed on Pepper, but I saw Coyote come up behind him when maybe no one else did. We found out later that Pepper's kidney got nicked, not enough to kill him, enough to look like it, though, and either way that shit was gonna hurt for a long time. But just like Pepper was there when Mikey2 later died on the third rail, that redheaded fuck never died but was always in the middle of some shit.

I told Mikey to wear a condom and hung up.

There was a baggie of weed under my mattress along with a red acrylic-tubed chrome pipe. I pinched some out and smoked up. I didn't really like getting high all that much, but if I was home alone and didn't have shit to do, there were worse things than being a little high and watching TV to pass the time.

Three's Company was on, but Chrissy was gone, and Old Man Roper had turned into Barney Fife, so I turned that shit off after about five minutes. I drank Pop's Stroh's and practiced Elvish letters from *The Silmarillion* for a while, then read *The Savage Sword of Conan* until the old man came home. I was halfway through "A Witch Shall Be Born" when the front door creaked open.

The old man popped into the living room, pretty buzzed. "Jeet?" he asked.

"No. Jew?"

"No. Squeet."

"S'go." I grinned at him.

This was a thing we did, maybe the best thing me and the old man did. If he came home drunk but in a good mood, we'd go out to eat.

"What's good, Pops? Where we grubbin'?" I asked.

"Why do you talk like that?" he asked, head shaking a little.

"Like what?"

"You know."

"Man, it is what it is. Ain't nothin'. It's how folks talk, know what I'm sayin'?"

"Like that," he said. "Shiiiiiit."

I for real didn't want to have a conversation about bigotry and whatnot, just wanted to go out to eat. He didn't even ask me about the big ol' bandage on my arm. He was funny that way. Either the nicest guy in the world or a truly mean son of a bitch. It depended on how much he drank. Tonight, he was kind of oddly right in between, a rare sweet spot. But yeah, folks in the bar loved him. Great storyteller, funny as fuck, bought drinks, great to be around. Everyone loved to see Teddy Sr. come through the door. But he really could only be that way when he was drinking. Had some bad shit happen to him when he was little, so if he wasn't drinking, he didn't talk. At all. Good thing he drank all the time, I guess. I never knew about the childhood stuff until way later, so trying to figure it out when I was a kid was fucked, and I had a hard time cutting him any slack. But that's always the deal with fathers and sons anyway, ain't it? Still, though, he owned up to it one day when we were drinking, in a story for another time.

Anyway.

"You want to know where we're eating?" he said.

"Yeah."

"The hillbilly place where I met your mother."

Oh shit, I said to myself. This mug been drinking more than I knew. And that restaurant was all the way over in Uptown.

"Alright, Pop. That's cool," I said. "How we getting there?"

His eyes barely focused on me.

"We're taking the El, dumbass."

U.S. DEPARTMENT OF JUSTICE

OFFICE OF PUBLIC AFFAIRS

FOR IMMEDIATE RELEASE   **Friday, March 4, 2022**

21 Alleged Gang Members and Associates Charged in RICO Indictment

Defendants' Charges Include Murder, Assault, Drug Trafficking, and Money Laundering

A federal indictment was unsealed today charging 21 alleged members and associates of the Simon City Royals gang with a racketeering conspiracy involving murder, attempted murder, narcotics trafficking, witness tampering, obstruction of justice, wire fraud and money laundering. . . . According to the indictment, the Simon City Royals are a national criminal gang whose dealings include extortion, narcotics, identity-theft, money laundering and violent crime. The gang has a formalized hierarchy involving numerous "boards" and "teams," including a team dedicated to carrying out violent gang punishments, and a "money team" responsible for earning revenue through fraud, illegal gambling, and identity theft.

And sometimes the gap swallows you, holds you, keeps you warm. Reminds you, binds you, swallowtails you in its folds. The city beats solid around you, forms to you even as it shapes your essence. You live together, forever, each for the other, a place made whole in the universe like none before or since. And sometimes its eyes make contact and look right through you but that's okay, you want it that way, the things you're seeing are things they never will, never should, couldn't know, even if they wanted to. I know most folks don't think it does, wouldn't believe it even if they seen it themselves, but spirit flows through Chicago streets like blood. Any alley, any avenue at magic hour, if you look just so, the right angle will show you pale blue sheet lightning writhing on oily water. That glow tells you you'll never be lost, will always be home. Your mother loves you, boys and girls. Don't ever forget.

ACKNOWLEDGMENTS

I wanted to write a story about taking the El. Just a short piece, something that would grab the rails, give the sights and sounds, write something that would let folks *feel* how much the El ran through our lives and let me relive the same. I *love* taking the train.

But once I got on the car? Those tracks took me right into this story and just kept going, everyone hopping in and telling their own. I did my best to hold on and get it all onto the page. This novel takes place over the course of a day, one of those last good ones of a summer at the end of a decade, and I think it shows how much can be happening in anyone's ride through the city. So thank you, CTA, for those big windows with plenty to look at and lots of space to think when I was growing up, riding you everywhere I could go. I owe you a little money for sneaking on at a couple of different stops bunches of times, but I figure the delays and broken heaters make us even.

Thanks as always to Amie, Emily, and Blue, especially for endlessly tolerating my talking about Chicago ✳ ✳ ✳ ✳. I'd say it gets worse when I'm writing stories set there, but that's not true. It's all the time.

To my supersmart and supportive editor, Anna Kaufman—thankyouthankyouthankyou for getting this book to do the things I knew it could eventually do, for encouraging creativity in its making (and the fight I'm sure you had with the production and typesetting folks), for giving me a shot, and for being you. Speaking of giving me a shot, my very best and bigbig thanks to agent extraordinaire Ron Eckel—you rock. Gen X ftw. The next one is on its way to you soon, sir.

Need to give big thanks to this honor roll of folks over at Vintage who worked so hard on this one: Nicole Pedersen, Annette Szlachta-McGinn, Tracy Gardstein, Conor O'Brien, Perry De La Vega, Christopher Zucker, Kali Maxwell, Kelsey Curtis, Maylin Lehmann Hobaica, and Natalia Berry. Wow. Thank you!

Many thanks to the Mackinac State Historic Parks Mackinac Island Artist-in-Residence Program for my time in our homelands to think about our ancestors as I finished this up. I'm forever grateful. Thanks as well to the Richard and Helen Phillips for the Tilikum Professorship and the accompanying support.

And finally, since this will be my fourth book set in my hometown, I've said hey to all the theaters, radio stations, diners, alleys, and folks who make it the greatest city in the world, so this one, believe it or not, shouts out the mighty Chicago Transit Authority, which, though it's seen better days and times, will no doubt return to its grimy, glorious self, getting folks mostly on time to all the amazing places in town they need to go, through the gift of public transportation.

During an interview for *Sacred City* the host asked me why I wrote these kinds of stories. I took a few seconds, got a little misty-eyed, and said, "'Cause I miss my friends."

I still do. Thanks for getting together again. See you later soon.